THE SURVIVALIST SAGA CONTINUES

Family. A family can consist of two individuals or millions but the number is inconsequential to its meaning. A family has a common goal, a reason to grow and to survive. We start off life depending on other members of this family to provide for our every need and then gradually, as we grow in both stature and intellect, we become the caregivers, worriers, the responsible ones. What happens when the ultimate "responsible one" is missing and not able to lead the family, to take it forward? John Rourke has disappeared, leaving no clue as to his whereabouts. There's already been one assassination attempt; could there have been another more successful one? It's not like he's the type of person who would run out of adversaries.

The virus spread by mutated insects is running rampant with a little or no survival rate. Political chaos and financial skullduggery spreads across this tattered and torn globe as well, fueled by Neo-Nazis and other unseen forces, edging in to manipulate the fate of the world. Bastions of democracy crumble, burying its allies under the rubble. Technology must take a step backward and a giant leap forward in order to gain a foothold.

The last few years have been on the quiet side and the Rourke clan is spending time on projects requiring less firepower, such as raising teenagers which, we find out, can prove very dangerous. Michael Rourke has some very tough decisions to make; some will affect his presidency and some will change the lives of family members. Life and death are all part of a family's cycle, even those whose lives span centuries.

Sharon

THE SURVIVALIST

#33

DEEP STAR

SPEAKING VOLUMES, LLC
NAPLES, FLORIDA
2015

THE SURVIVALIST
#33 DEEP STAR

ISBN 978-1-62815-285-2

**For more exciting
Books, eBooks, Audiobooks and more visit us at
www.speakingvolumes.us**

THE SURVIVALIST

#33

DEEP STAR

Jerry Ahern
Sharon Ahern
Bob Anderson

To

John R.S. Anderson and Mike Spinella, two faithful readers.
Life has a way of happening and sometimes,
you are simply along for the ride.
Continue to <u>Plan Ahead</u>!

"Sometimes I wonder whether the world is being run
by smart people who are putting us on or
by imbeciles who really mean it." —Mark Twain

Prologue

The Hall of Records stood empty for the first time in centuries. It had served its purpose with distinction. John Rourke smiled at Sanderson and slapped Akiro on the back. "A double success guys, recovery of the artifacts and successful abatement of centuries of ice and snow from one of our nation's greatest monuments. It is a great day."

"Yes, it is," Kuriname said, still unable to shake the sense of foreboding.

Rourke's satellite phone cheeped. "Go ahead," he said.

Back in Hawaii, Paul Rubenstein and Randall Walls had been watching for "patterns" of activity around Mount Rushmore. Paul said, "You have incoming. ETA fifteen minutes, maybe ten. Evacuate to the southeast. Rally at Point Victor for extraction. I repeat, Point Victor."

"Roger," Rourke said into the radio, then turned to Sanderson and Akiro Kuriname, "Damnit! Get everything moving, we have company inbound. Load everybody up. Wes contact the VTOLs and tell them to launch and move to Point Victor, we'll meet them there. Any equipment not already loaded on the ATPAAVs, leave it. We have to leave now. Tell your drivers to make it to Point Victor for extraction."

Rourke watched the loading process and took a last look around; discarded equipment littered the area. Rourke ran to the juncture of the glacier; a Viking ATPAAV slid to a stop next to him. "Get in Mr. Rourke," a muffled voice called out.

"Thanks for the lift, let's move out." The driver stepped on the gas and rocketed across the ice. The other ATPAAVs charged ahead of them; already over a half mile distant and appearing to be pulling away from them. Rourke shouted into the wind. "Go! Go! You have to catch up to them."

Realizing the gap to the other Vikings was increasing, Rourke shouted, "Step on it, damn it!" A hundred yards in front of them the snow suddenly exploded and Rourke lost sight of the other vehicles as more energy bolts flashed from the sky. Hanging onto the overhead roof cage, Rourke turned to his right and looked behind; two silver objects streaked toward them belching green energy bursts. Rourke watching, shouted, "Turn! You have to go right, damn it and step on it. We have to catch up; the VTOLs won't wait on us."

Suddenly, the vehicle slowed, and then stopped. Rourke looked at the driver, shouting, "What the hell..." The driver's left hand held a pistol pointed at Rourke's chest. "I'm counting on the VTOLs not waiting for us, Mr. Rourke." An energy blast hit nearby, throwing snow and ice on them just as Rourke pulled his Sting 1A boot knife and lunged. The driver squeezed the trigger just as the wave of concussion violently rocked the ATPAAV onto its side, throwing both men out.

Rourke rolled through the impact, landing on his back, with the Sting still clutched in his right hand. He scrambled to his feet just as the driver leapt at him; Rourke's left hand closed on the man's throat as the impact sent them rolling. Rourke ended up on top, his grip tightened and the man's face began turning red. Rourke stabbed down at the man's face with the double-edged boot knife but his assailant's left hand caught Rourke's wrist in mid thrust.

Sharp pain suddenly stabbed through Rourke's chest; his strength faded and his grip loosened. The driver coughed violently and shoved Rourke over and off of him. Rourke tried to move but couldn't. He thought, *I'm dying.* Able to move only his eyes, he saw a hypodermic sticking out of his chest. Rourke's world started spinning as his attacker stood over him and he noticed the man's name tag for the first time— ARNOLD.

Why? Rourke's mind framed the question silently as darkness took him completely.

Chapter One

It has been said that, "birds of a feather flock together." This is particularly true of vultures. William Alan Davis stands five foot, ten inches tall. He's intelligent, charismatic, erudite and nice looking in a collegiate sort of way. One early acquaintance described him as "kind, solicitous, and empathetic;" all traits he exploited in winning the trust of his young female victims.

As an adolescent, he had "experimented" with dogs and cats from the neighborhood. For years, neighborhood pets would disappear from time to time. The first few were found; dissected. Two cats were found that had been set on fire. It caused such a stink that young Davis decided he must hide the bodies of his victims.

A nearby wooded area had become his "cemetery." For years, he perfected his game. He would spot a target, figure out how to make the snatch and then stalk the animal until he made the snatch. During this period of his life, he had been able to fulfill his sick fantasies on cats and dogs. Eventually, he realized he was not getting the same "kick" that he used to get during his stalks, captures and killings.

The next evolution took place on his first human murder. His killing spree began in full force. He would often revisit his secondary crime scenes for hours at a time, grooming and performing sexual acts with the decomposing corpses until putrefaction and destruction by wild animals made further interaction impossible.

A serial killer, rapist, kidnapper, and a necrophile, he approaches his victims in public places, feigning injury or disability, or impersonating an authority figure, before overpowering and assaulting them at more secluded locations.

Lee Elwood McAllen, neither intelligent, charismatic nor nice looking, is also a serial killer and rapist... and a cannibal. Just less than six feet with a crooked gap-toothed smile he seldom exhibited except to his victims, he shows signs of moderate mental retardation, with an I.Q. of only seventy-five.

The two met at a soup kitchen where they developed a sort of Mutt and Jeff relationship; Davis was the leader and the brains, McAllen, the follower and the muscle.

They were "sadistic sociopaths," taking pleasure from another human's pain and the control they had over victims; to the point of death, and beyond. Davis once described himself "as the most cold-hearted son of a bitch you'll ever meet." One psychiatric staff member called him, "the very definition of heartless evil."

At the moment, they were merely stalking; hunting. They had been on the hunt for the past three days and the sexual tension of hunting was reaching a fever pitch in both, a condition known to be a form of Paraphilia. Hunting dominated their every waking moment until a target was found.

They had found their new targets and sat in the old van chain smoking. "There," Davis said. "There they are." He smiled and punched McAllen on the shoulder.

McAllen lit up a joint, flashed that crooked gap-toothed grin saying, "Yeah, they're purdy." McAllen would also be diagnosed as suffering from paranoid schizophrenia, but this would not happen until the trial of the century was launched.

Chapter Two

The evacuation from Mount Rushmore had gone well. Unfortunately, it wasn't until the VTOL transports had lifted off, that the horrible truth was realized. Chief Warrant Officer, Wes Sanderson, was the first to realize it. After a roll-call with the other planes, he learned that John Rourke was not on any of them. He had seen Bennett Arnold pick Rourke up and begin the drive to rally at Point Victor; neither ever arrived. Sanderson had motioned to Akiro to come to the rear of the plane. "Akiro, Rourke is not on board any of the planes, and neither is your guy Arnold."

Akiro was stunned. "Are you sure? You've talked to the other planes?"

"Just got through, neither made it to the pickup point. I thought in all of the confusion and haste they made it on one of the other birds but they didn't. I saw your man Arnold with Rourke in his ATPAAV as we left Rushmore. On the way, I noticed they were a little behind the rest of us but I figured they had caught up."

"Arnold?" Kuriname pondered. "That's the guy I wanted you to help me watch."

"I know," Sanderson said. "I watched him during the excavation of Rushmore and loading of the artifacts and he seemed okay but, when the attack occurred, I... I lost sight of him until we were evacuating."

Akiro closed his eyes and bowed his head; he said, "Son of a bitch," barely above a whisper. "We have to call this in... now!" He stood and with Sanderson following went to the ladder going up the flight deck.

The Crew Chief stopped them. "Can I help you Gentlemen?"

Kuriname said, "We have to speak with the pilot, now Chief. Right now. It is imperative we speak to Colonel Ball. He's on one of the other transports."

*****

"General Sullivan... I don't know how to say this," Colonel "Mad Jack" Ball said into the microphone.

General Sullivan responded quickly, "Spit it out, Colonel."

Ball took a deep breath. "John Rourke and one of Kuriname's men did not make the pickup."

Sullivan said nothing for a long moment. "What the hell are you saying?"

"The mission was closing down and everything was moving according to the plan when we were advised of incoming craft. We headed to Point Victor for pickup. Things got pretty hairy real quick. When we got to Point Victor, our men and the scientists got on the first transports they were able to. First come, first serve... Once we were airborne, we did a head count and that's when we realized we were two short."

"I've rechecked with all of the other planes. Rourke is not aboard any of them, nor is one of Kuriname's men, a guy named Bennett Arnold..." It was all Ball could do to force out the next words. "Arnold and John Rourke are both missing. Missing and, at this point, they have to be presumed captured or dead. Sir, Rourke is gone."

"Missing and presumed dead... Arnold and Rourke... gone?" Sullivan mumbled to himself then was silent for a long moment and then said, "Well, your conclusion is unacceptable."

Ball looked at the microphone. "Sir?"

"A conclusion is the place where you got tired of thinking, Colonel." Sullivan's briskness caught Ball by surprise.

4

"Huh?"

"You're not done thinking, get back to it. I want answers and a plan; I can't have the second until I have the first, so get back to thinking. I want answers and I want them fast..."

Chapter Three

Paula Rourke and Natalie Rubenstein walked two steps in front of their brothers, Tim Rourke and John "Jack" Michael Rubenstein. Paula, the oldest by a few months, said, "I don't know why we had to bring them. They are such..."

Natalie supplied the word. "Boys?"

"Yes... boys," Paula said and laughed.

Tim said, "We didn't want to come with you two either."

Jack said, "Yeah, we don't need babysitters." The four were headed to Benny's and Bubba's Eatery and Arcade. Benny's and Bubba's had become a Mecca for young families needing a night out, young kids and teenagers looking for a place to hang. There were so many different interesting fun activities that "you could get lost before you get started!" On a Half Off Wednesday, ten dollars will get you forty-eight credits and one of the games cost ten credits. Plus Benny's and Bubba's was famous for "good deals," you pay twenty dollars and you get twenty dollars in extra credits, around two-hundred and fifty.

Benny's and Bubba's was known for having a casino atmosphere for kids of all ages without the "dangers of gambling." The arcade has plenty of games like spin-the-wheel or watch a light circle around and then push the button to stop the light. But, there's also the Wheel of Fortune game that can be quite pricey. Plus there was the Go-Kart game that was fun, all the rest were shooter and driving games. It was a great place to waste an hour or the afternoon.

The kids stopped at the front desk first to get their cards, that was the key to unlocking "an action-packed, extreme-fun experience," as the ads said. You could charge it up to play every game in the arcade area. It could also earn you exciting tokens and tickets that got you a discount on meals or another round at the games which numbered over two hundred different arcade machines.

Jack slid his card into the breast pocket of his yellow button up shirt. "Okay," he said turning to the girls. "You guys just want to eat and talk girl stuff, and try to pick up boys. Go have fun. Tim and I are headed to the arcade to play the games."

In the three food areas, appetizers, not to mention a full menu featuring burgers, steaks, seafood, pasta and salads were available. Even the most discriminating customer was "sure to find something satisfying." It is considered the safest, fun place in town.

None of them had seen the handsome young man exit the old van across the street and follow them inside, or the older man who remained in the van.

Chapter Four

Davis watched the girls order their meals and then waited until they took possession of two of the remaining unoccupied seats in the dining area. He shyly approached them, limping noticeably. "Excuse me, all of the tables are filled. Would you ladies mind if I just sit here for a minute and eat my snack?" He held up a rumbled brown paper bag. "I won't be a problem, I promise. I twisted my ankle a couple of days ago and it still hurts."

Natalie smiled. "How did you twist it?" She gestured to the empty chair across from them.

Davis smiled a boyish grin. "I tripped and fell in a hole." He took a sandwich from his bag, an unopened can of soda and a partially opened bag of potato chips. Biting into the sandwich he mumbled, "Have you heard about that archaeological dig up on North Shore? I was removing some artifacts, tripped over a shovel handle and fell back into the dig."

Intrigued, Paula leaned forward, "The old village they found... you're involved with that?"

He nodded. "Graduate student... research for my dissertation. You guys freshmen at U of H?"

Natalie thought, *He's both handsome and an older man;* the thought tickled her fancy. *After all, nothing could happen in Benny's and Bubba's.* She smiled. "Yes, first semester."

Paula frowned but went along with the game. It was just a game and, *after all, nothing could happen in Benny's and Bubba's.* "No," she said. "I'm at Mid-Wake U, just home for a visit."

The waiter approached, carrying the tray. "Okay, ladies... double cheese burger with onion rings and sweetened tea?" Paula raised her hand and the waiter placed her meal down. In front of Natalie he sat the

Caesar Salad, two sticks of buttery garlic bread and a diet soda. "Anything for the gentleman?"

Davis had ducked below the table to hide his face from the waiter. "No thanks; thanks anyway." Once the waiter left, he sat back up. "Sorry about that, I had to tie my shoe, don't want to trip on the shoelace," he laughed. "I can't afford another injury." His smile was easy and relaxing. "I'm C. J."

The girls introduced themselves and began eating. For the next hour "C.J." regaled them with his exploits on various archaeological dig projects; projects that had never existed.

Chapter Five

The woman who had tried to kidnap John Rourke in the car ambush sat in the interview room across from Tim Shaw, rubbing the heavy bandages that covered her right hand and extended halfway up her arm. Her eyes lowered as if studying the table between them. The single, long blond braid hung over her right shoulder, almost to her waist. Shaw thought, *She is a beauty, if a lethal one.*

"Here's what we know right now," Shaw said. "Admittedly, it is not much. From all indications you are in your early thirties. Your fingerprints aren't in any of our data banks. That leads me to believe you are not American, even though your speech patterns and accent are flawless."

She smiled demurely.

"We have forwarded your prints to the CIA, NSA and INTERPOL. I suspect you're European, although you might be Russian. The submachine gun we recovered is a Russian model. We have been more fortunate concerning data regarding your companion," Shaw said, flipping open the file that he then placed on the table. "His prints identify him a Harvey Donaldson, local muscle for hire; spent some time as a mercenary and linked to organized crime."

Finally, she looked up at him. "You were honest at least, you don't know much. Look, this thing itches." She indicated the bandage. "Call one of your doctors, the itch is maddening."

"The doctors say that is part of the normal healing process, Miss..." She said nothing.

"Okay, why did you attack John Rourke?"

"I didn't attack him, he attacked us. My companion, Harvey, is dead and I may well be maimed for life. I'm the victim here."

"Why were you after Dr. Rourke? Look," Shaw said with finality, "I'm not going to sit here with you wasting time. I don't believe it will be long before we know who you are and who you're working for. Now is the time to talk... Once we have that information, what you say will be of... less value to me. Help yourself while you still have the chance."

She turned in her chair, her deep blue eyes locked with Shaw's dark brown ones. Then she laughed. "Alright! Why not... you're right, it should not take long for you to find out who I am. But you are completely mistaken about my actions."

"Really," Shaw said with a raised eyebrow.

"I wasn't trying to kill John Rourke, I was trying to save his life. I wasn't trying to kidnap him; I was trying to get him into... protective custody. You are partially correct; there are people that want him dead. However, I'm not one of them. My name is Arin Ágústsson; I am a special assistant to the Yfirlögregluþjónn, what you would call the Detective Chief Superintendent of the Icelandic National Police."

Taking a deep breath, she slumped in the chair. "I am here on his special orders. The people of Iceland still feel a tremendous debt to Dr. Rourke. He brought us into the new world after the old one died."

"Why the ambush, Arin?"

She smiled. "John Rourke has a reputation for being somewhat... impulsive. My instructions were to isolate and contain him; quickly. Once we had him peacefully in our custody, we could have explained the dangers he was in. We knew there wasn't much time to make contact, but not how receptive Mr. Rourke would be to our imperatives. His cooperation was not viewed as important as his preservation."

Shaw flipped to his report. "Seems you told Rourke, and I quote, 'I'd prefer not to have to shoot you. That being said, I also believe I have no compunction in pulling the trigger if you do not comply.' Is that accurate?"

She looked down at the table between them and took a long, slow, deep breath. "Yes, the first part is accurate but I did not want to shoot him. The second part was a bluff. My orders were to get him safely into custody as soon as possible. I would not have shot him. My options were limited by my instructions from the Yfirlögregluþjónn; 'Make it quick and make it quiet but make him safe.'"

Shaw smirked. "Yeah, and how did that work out for you?"

She held up her wounded hand. "Not very damn well, obviously. Look, I was chosen for this mission because I am a descendent of Sigrid Jokli, who was our Madam President at the time of Rourke's first visit to my country."

"That was, what... a hundred and fifty or so years ago?" Shaw asked.

"Yes, that is close enough," she said. "Rourke met Bjorn Rolvaag and his dog outside Lydveldid Island during a rescue mission for his daughter who had been kidnapped. It led to the meeting between my ancestor and the Rourkes, and that led to John Rourke moving my country from the idyllic isolationism we had enjoyed since the Night of the War, into the modern world."

Chapter Six

Emma dialed Michael Rourke's private number but was shuttled to some unidentified underling in Michael's office. She told the man, "My husband, John Rourke, was late for a scheduled check-in call and didn't make it. Now he is late for another one; understand? He's late again."

"I'm sorry Mrs. Rourke but, as I said, the President is currently unavailable."

"Did you tell him that it was me?" She asked, the frustration coming through clearly in her voice.

"Ma'am, I'm not at liberty to say anymore."

She heard a vehicle pull up in the drive and said disgustedly, "Very well, thank you for your help and total lack of information." Hanging hung up the phone she walked to the front door. Glancing out a window she saw a Highway Patrol vehicle. *Strange,* she thought as she opened the door. "Can I help you?"

"Mrs. Rourke," the Sergeant said. "Is your husband home?" The Corporal with him stood silent and solemn.

Thinking he wanted to talk about the attempt on John's life by the blond and the man with the shotgun, she said, "No, he is... out of the country at the moment, can I help you?"

"Mrs. Rourke... Uh, Mrs. Rourke, I'm afraid there has been an incident. May I come in?"

Emma opened the door. "Of course, what kind of incident?"

The Sergeant took a deep breath and said softly, "Mrs. Rourke... There is no easy way to tell you. We have a report that your son and daughter may have been kidnapped."

Emma sat down on a vacant chair in the hallway used to sit at while changing shoes in inclement weather or dropping book bags on after school. "I have to make a phone call." Shaking, she dialed a number. "Dad, get over here right now, hurry please!" She hung up and called the Rubensteins; Paul answered.

"Emma, are you alright?"

"No, I'm not!" She screamed. "Have you heard from the kids?"

"HPD just drove up. We just found out ourselves. Stay there, I'm on my way to you."

Chapter Seven

The Detective Sergeant installed a "trace and trap" tap on the Rubenstein's home phone, and pulled two cell phones from his case. "I need one of you to stay here in case the kidnappers call. Here, you two can use these to stay in touch with each other."

Hugging Annie, Paul kissed her forehead and said, "I'm going to Emma's."

"Give Emma my love," Annie said.

"I'll be right back," Paul said and ran outside and jumped into his car. He pulled into the Rourke driveway a split second before Tim Shaw slid to a tire-screeching halt in the street.

"Paul," Tim shouted. "What's going on?"

"Come on Tim, hurry." The two sprinted to the front door; Paul barreled in with Shaw behind him. Tim saw the Patrolmen, flashed his credential case, bellowing, "What the hell is going on?"

Emma sat rocking her baby son, Eddie; named after her brother. Tears stained her face and light blue blouse. "Oh Dad, our kids... our kids... someone has our kids." Emma turned to Paul for the first time, recognizing the agony on his face.

Paul nodded. "Ours too. Tim, they have our kids."

Shaw pulled his radio, keyed the mic and said, "This is Shaw. Get in touch with POTUS... I don't give a shit who he's meeting with. Tell him to call me immediately at John Rourke's home. I want a level three security blanket on POTUS, the First Lady and their kids, right now! Locate them all and secure them and let me know when it's done. Tell POTUS I'm waiting on his call... Just do it. Don't ask me any more questions damn it! Just follow your damn orders."

Shaw broke the connection, took a deep breath and walked over to Emma. He kissed his daughter on her head and took his grandson from her arms. "Come here, Little Eddie, you little angel..." He looked at Emma and smiled, but it was a hollow smile. He had never seen such a picture of such abject agony as he saw on the face of his daughter.

Chapter Eight

There was a knock on the door of Michael Rourke's office. He looked up angrily when the Marine Guard walked to his desk and handed the President a note. "I'm sorry to interrupt Mr. President."

Michael opened the note; he read it through twice, then a third time. He felt a block of ice forming around his heart as he stood and faced the window. Slowly he turned around. "Ladies and Gentlemen, I'm afraid I must stop this meeting. My apologies, but it can't be helped. I will have my office contact each of you and reschedule this as soon as possible. I'm afraid I have to ask you to leave now, I have an emergency."

The Marine Guard turned to escort the members of Michael's Cabinet out. Michael said, "Mr. Attorney General, I'm asking you to please stand by. I have a private phone call I have to make." He told the Guard, "I need the Directors of the FBI and the NSA in my office, immediately."

"I'll be right outside your office, Mr. President," the AG said.

Michael nodded his thanks, sat down heavily and dialed Tim Shaw's number. "Shaw here, Mr. President... I hope you're sitting down and alone."

"I am, Tim." These were the last sane words he said for the next fifteen minutes.

Chapter Nine

The snatch was going off without a hitch. Davis asked the girls if they wanted to see some "really cool artifacts we found." Paula and Natalie had jumped on the idea. They found the boys and waited for them to finish their last game. Natalie said, "Come on guys, this is C.J. and he has some neat stuff to show us. He's an archaeologist."

Tim looked at Jack, both of them were frowning. Jack was the first to speak up, "I don't know..." he started to say.

C.J. smiled with a laugh. "Come on guys, I've got something for you two also." They walked outside and crossed the street to the van. McAllen had been watching the door to Benny's and Bubba's; seeing Davis, he left the vehicle and stood against a wall by the van. He looked like just another homeless guy on the street.

Davis/C.J. twisted the door handle on the sliding side door. "Come on girls. Look in the back, there's even a gold headband..." Reaching into his front pants pocket, he pulled out a small aerosol container about the size of a breath spray and took a deep breath which he held. When the girls leaned in, Davis hit them both with the spray and flipped them into the van.

At that instant McAllen exploded into motion and shoved the boys between their shoulder blades as hard as he could into the van. Jack hollered, "Hey..." and started screaming "Help, help us..."

Tim got to his knees, turned and swung a punch at Davis. Davis slapped him across the mouth with a backhanded swat that sent Tim flying into a side wall; stunned. Davis took another deep breath and hit both boys with the knockout spray as he climbed in and moved to the driver's seat and cranked the motor.

McAllen slammed the sliding door and jerked open the passenger door and jumped in.

Two men, driving a pickup, saw the attack. The driver slammed on the brakes and pulled in front of the van and jumped out. He shouted, "Hey, what the hell is going on?" His passenger ran to McAllen's door and tried to open it.

McAllen hit him in the mouth, the man flew backwards landing on his back; his head slamming into the concrete curb... He laid still, very still. McAllen shouted, "Let's go. Let's go." Davis slammed the van into drive and spun the steering wheel hard to the left. The pickup driver dove out of the way; he hit the hard concrete road on his right shoulder, tearing his shirt and ripping the skin on his shoulder; he kept rolling out of the way.

Jumping up, he started running after the van. Running hard and fast, he saw the signal light ahead turn red. He ran even harder. *Now I've got 'em,* he thought.

Davis looked both ways and jammed the accelerator to the floor, tires screeching and smoking. He shot ahead trying to make it between an off-green, four-door sedan coming from the right and a city garbage truck coming from the left. The sedan, loaded with a mother and two kids, slammed on its brakes and fishtailed before coming to a stop.

The garbage truck driver locked up his brakes; tires squealed and smoked. He clipped the left rear fender of the van, spinning it to the left. Davis saw he was going to be hit and turned into the impact. Metal crunched, the left rear hubcap flew off. Davis cursed and stomped the peddle once again. Burning rubber, he took off in that new direction. In seconds, he was gone.

The runner slowed and stopped, watching helplessly as the van disappeared up the street. He ran to the sidewalk, jerked a cell phone out of the hand of a man dressed in a business suit and quickly dialed 911.

Breathlessly, he said, "Kidnapping... kids snatched... older white van... driver white... last three of the license... 677... Hawaii plate," then slumped to the ground.

Catching his breath he handed the phone back and looked around for his friend, but his passenger was nowhere in sight. Down the street, he saw his friend lying on the sidewalk, not moving.

He ran back, a pool of dark red/black blood forming a halo around his friend's head. He checked for a pulse, it was weak. The business man had followed him and was giving information to the 911 operator. "We need police and an ambulance in front of Benny's and Bubba's. A man is hurt... hurry, please hurry."

Sirens could be heard in the distance.

Chapter Ten

Tim Shaw was angry and frustrated as he sat listening to the Police Captain on the patio in back of Emma and John's house. Captain Jim Walker was six foot, four inches tall and two hundred, forty pounds. With his black tactical uniform, his shaven head and spit shine boots, he looked like he had been carved from a gigantic piece of polished ebony. "Here's what we know," Walker said.

"We know that the kids walked out of Benny's and Bubba's freely. We have video of them exiting; a white man was with them. A check of the videos show that he followed them in. Problem is either he was damned lucky or he knew where the cameras were, we didn't get a picture of his face; a camera across the street got a partial."

"He had a partner waiting across the street by the van. He also avoided the cameras; no luck there, either. Two eyewitnesses tried to intervene; one chased the van for almost two blocks on foot. He couldn't get a make, but we know it was an older model van, white, and the last three digits of the Hawaiian license plate are 677. We're running that."

"The other eyewitness was injured; he's in ICU at General, still touch and go with him. His skull cracked when he hit the street. Traffic camera at the intersection snapped this when the driver busted the red light." He slid a black and white photo across the table. "Clean shot of the driver and we have identified him as William Alan Davis; white male, five feet, ten inches tall, twenty-three years old. That's all we have, so far..."

Shaw asked, "What about the other man?"

Ben Phillips, commander of the FBI Hostage Rescue team, was the exact opposite of Walker. Only about five foot ten, his head sported a short buzz cut of shockingly white stubble. His body was wiry and tight, energy vibrated around him. He said, "We think we know his partner's name. Davis has been seen in the company of a Lee Elwood McAllen, late twenties or early thirties, just under six feet tall. McAllen has crooked teeth and is gap toothed on the top. His medical records show he has signs of moderate mental retardation. He is illiterate and suffers from epilepsy and grand mal seizures. The two allegedly met at a soup kitchen where they developed a sort of relationship."

"We think Davis is the leader and McAllen is the follower. We think the injured witness tried to stop the kidnapping and ran to the passenger side of the van where McAllen slugged him. McAllen's punch slammed him back, landing on the back of his head, cracking his skull open. McAllen has a similar van registered to him, but the last three digits on the plate are 643. Might be stolen plates or could be the guy that chased the van... what was his name?"

The Captain said, "Dylan Wilson, construction worker."

"Yeah, maybe Wilson got the number wrong, mistakes happen," Phillips said.

Walker said, "We're checking theft reports now, but if the plates are stolen the owner may not even know it yet."

Shaw took a sip of now cold coffee, and pulled a cigarette pack from his pocket. The damn thing was empty; Shaw needed a cigarette. He crumpled the empty pack and cursed. "Damnit, anybody got a smoke?"

Phillips fished in his breast pocket and flipped a pack of Camels to Shaw. "Take it easy Mr. Shaw; you need a little anger management right now."

That was all it took to set Shaw off. "Hell, I don't need anger management. I need people to stop pissing me off! My people skills are just fine. It's my tolerance to idiots that needs work." He lit the cigarette and took a deep draw on it. "Now, what do we know about the perps."

"Quite a bit, actually," the Captain said seriously as he consulted a file. "Both have had a couple of minor scrapes with the law; petty theft, simple assault, stuff like that. McAllen... well, there are reports of him being a serial arsonist as a child; he got off on fire. We're getting their juvenile records sent over. Looks like his childhood was a nightmare, his mother was a religious fanatic. He claims that she abused him, exposed him to various Satanic practices and rituals in his youth, including self-mutilation and grave robbing."

Chapter Eleven

While Davis' concoction was fast acting, it didn't last long. Tim was the first to start waking up. Groggy, his face and head hurt from Davis' backhand slap that had sent him flying into the side wall of the van. He laid on his right side; his left cheek, red and tender. The left eye puffed up into what would become a world class black eye.

His hands were wrapped in duct tape and a gag, now soaked in his own saliva, plugged his mouth. He remained still, watching out of his good right eye as his sister and cousins stirred. Like him they were duct taped, gagged and lying on their sides. Paula came around first, then Jack and finally Natalie. Paula looked around confused. Natalie looked scared and Jack... Jack looked mad.

Paula looked wide eyed at Tim; he smiled, or tried to and winked. She winked back, she was okay. Natalie had tears running down her cheeks. Jack grimaced and tried to pull his hands free but couldn't. Tim got Jack's eyes and shook his head. Jack took a deep breath and stopped struggling.

Tim thought to himself, *Okay, we're in trouble. But everyone looks okay. At least for now.*

The others looked at him; he closed his eyes and tilted his head like he was asleep. Then he opened his eyes wide and looked hard at them and repeated the motion. Paula nodded and mimicked him and then she opened her eyes and nodded her head. Tim nodded back and she repeated the motion and stayed "asleep" this time.

Natalie watched and figured it out; she "went to sleep." Jack looked at Tim; Tim repeated the silent instruction, he had to do it twice before Jack nodded his agreement and closed his eyes. Tim looked around one last time; the inside of the van was bare, nothing he could use. C.J. and the other man sat up front facing forward. Tim thought, *We have to wait for an opportunity... or we have to wait for someone to find us.*

Then he closed his eyes and feigned sleep.

Chapter Twelve

Walker told Shaw, "McAllen ran away from home, but he was brought back. Later he claimed he was forced to have sex with a friend of his father's when he was five years old. By age ten, he decided he was homosexual. Claims to have had a consensual relationship with a neighbor boy when he was twelve. He dropped out of school in the ninth grade and began visiting gay bars. He says he was a male prostitute as a teenager, his first arrest was at the age of seventeen."

"He drifted around, supporting himself by prostitution and panhandling. He was one of the prime suspects in the murder of a twenty-four year old college student. Later he was named a 'person of interest' in the murder of a thirty-one year old housewife but he disappeared and showed up here."

"Davis, on the other hand, has a college education. He was born in a home for unwed mothers, in..." He checked the records. "Texas. The identity of his father has never been determined with certainty. Some of his relatives believe his father was actually his own mother's violent and abusive father. There is no existing evidence to prove that, however. His birth certificate lists him as a 'bastard.'"

"He did the psycho triad; bed wetting, fire starting and cruelty to animals. There is an early report that during a time when he was living with his grandparents, the grandmother woke one day from a nap to find herself surrounded by knives from the kitchen and her grandson standing by the bed, smiling."

"His high school and college class mates called him bright but withdrawn. Teenage drinking got him in trouble several times, and there are a number of field interview cards where he was caught out late at night. The police suspected he was looking for undraped windows where he could observe women undressing, or whatever." Captain Walker closed the file report.

Shaw drug his hand over the stubble on his chin. "This just keeps getting better, doesn't it?" He mumbled under his breath and stretched his right leg out. "Damn, I hate it when my foot falls asleep during the day 'cause that means it's gonna be up all night."

Walker said, "Tim, you're talking to yourself. What is it?"

Shaw looked up surprised. "Of course I talk to myself, sometimes I need expert advice. Never mind, I'm just thinking out loud."

In times of stress, Shaw used his Wrightisms more than normal. Steven Wright was an old American comedian Shaw had discovered in some of John Rourke old tapes. Shaw thought Wright's distinctly lethargic voice and slow, deadpan delivery of ironic, philosophical and sometimes nonsensical jokes, fit his own personality. "What about Davis?"

The Captain shrugged. "He's as dangerous as McAllen, probably worse. He has been interviewed several times as a suspect in the disappearance of young women. He showed up here two years ago." Walker said, "I suspect we have a team now, made up of these two losers; a pair of serial rapists if not serial killers. I know we have a hell of a problem and we better solve it quick, the clock is ticking. The kids were snatched; he pulled up his sleeve to check his watch... two hours and twenty-five minutes ago."

Shaw nodded. "We both know the numbers. The bad news is in nearly sixty percent of cases, more than two hours usually pass between the time someone realized the child was missing and the time police were notified. The good news is our search began almost immediately."

The Captain agreed. "Another bit of good news, traffic cams recorded an older model van with new damage to the left rear quarter panel, after the accident. Our technicians are monitoring footage from all over town, trying to locate it. Bad news is... nothing yet. Shaw, you know as well as I do that in seventy-six percent of the missing children homicide cases, the child is dead within three hours of the abduction. In almost ninety percent of the cases, the child is dead within twenty-four hours. After the first forty-eight hours following an abduction, the chance of finding the victim or in this case the victims alive is, for all intent, virtually unheard of."

Shaw nodded, "Yeah, I know. Over a thousand people go missing every day and we have no way of knowing how long these two had been active. They know how to rape and murder; probably have been getting away with it for some time."

Phillips said, "My HRT is the best counter-terrorism and hostage rescue unit the FBI has. I can tell you we're good at what we do. We're trained specifically to rescue citizens in hostage and high-risk law enforcement situations. I have fifty of our best operators headed this way." He checked his watch. "The last team should arrive in about forty minutes."

Captain Walker said, "Look, we're not going to get into a turf pissing war with you guys. While normally we would have jurisdiction, the fact that these victims are part of the Rourke family changes everything. We will cooperate fully with the Bureau."

Shaw said, "Thank you Captain. Guys, here is my bottom line. These aren't just victims; they happen to be my... Two of them are my grandchildren and the other two are their cousins. You have the unlimited resources of the Secret Service. The only good piece of news is John Thomas Rourke is currently out of the country and you have to deal with me instead of him. You may think I'm a son of a bitch, and I am. But if this goes down wrong, you will be dealing with him and John Rourke scares the hell outta me."

Chapter Thirteen

Tim Rourke lay there... thinking, *What can we do?* He thought about his father, *Plan ahead, that's what Dad always says.* A sharp pain stabbed in his side. Raising himself up a little, he saw a rusty nail head protruding a quarter of an inch out of the floor. They had been taken, not too gently, out of the van and were now in a room; a dirty and dark and damp room, and he didn't have a clue as to where it was located. He did know that they didn't have much time left. He lay back down and bumped his head gently on the floor to catch the other's attention. Then he rolled onto his back and slowly pushed both feet out and up; he looked at them and did it again, faster this time.

They nodded and then Tim closed his eyes and laid his head back down. They all went "back to sleep" and waited. Tim began to work the nail head quietly on the duct tape that bound his hands. When it finally parted enough, he rested. He was about to free Jack when he heard the floor creak. *They're coming,* he thought. He lay there keeping his hands behind him as if they were still bound.

Tim lay still as Davis approached with McAllen close behind. He and Jack were closest and lay curled up in fetal positions. Davis went to the girls to check them and he said with some concern, "They should be awake by now."

"Yeah," McAllen said as he reached for Jack. Jack rolled over on his back and shot out both legs, smacking McAllen in the face as he leaned over. "Damn it," McAllen screamed as he staggered back. Tim rolled over and launched his feet at McAllen's crotch. "Oooooh," McAllen squealed as he sank to his knees.

Paula's feet shot out aiming for Davis' face; he swatted them away. Natalie's feet smashed into his right ankle and Davis fell. "Bitch," he shouted and struck Natalie's jaw hard with his fist. Paula tried again and missed again.

Davis turned his attention to her. Tim pushed up from the floor and got his legs under him and jumped, aiming for Davis and hitting him in small of the back. The impact sent them both tumbling. Tim kept punching at Davis' head as hard as he could.

McAllen stood up and pulled a small blue steel revolver from his belt. "Stop it! Stop it! Stop it now," he shouted. The kids froze. McAllen helped Davis to his feet. "You okay?"

Davis flashed a glare of pure hate that scanned the face of each of the kids, before slugging Tim in the face. "Yeah, I'm alright but they aren't." He looked into Paula's eyes. "I'm going to take my time with you," he said before looking at Natalie. "And you too, and when I'm through with you, I'm gonna kill ya and then rape you again and again. After you're dead, you little whores... I'll let the rats feed on you. By the time your bodies are found... Well, it won't be an open casket funeral, I promise. Oh, by the way, Lee really likes boys; want to know what's in store for you?"

McAllen smiled that crooked gap-toothed grin. "Let me tell, can I tell them?"

Davis smiled. "Sure."

McAllen looked at Tim. "You're first, I'm lookin' forward to you." He looked over at Jack. "And when I'm through with him, you'll be next. When I'm through with both of ya, I'm going to strangle you with my bare hands." He licked his lips. "Then ya know what I'm gonna do? I'm going to slice ya up and cook ya for my supper, hahahaha!"

Davis slapped Paula across the face. "Bring me some rope for this one," he said, pointing at Tim. McAllen went in the next room and returned with a small length of grass rope. Davis rebound Tim's hands and threw him across the room. "Come on," he said to McAllen. Davis wiped blood from his jaw. "I need to see how bad this cut is, that little bastard..." He looked at Tim. "You guys enjoy yourselves for a little while. Trust me, you ain't going anywhere and we'll be back shortly."

Chapter Fourteen

Paul and Annie had just checked in with each other and Paul told her he would be on his way back shortly. Captain Walker approached Rubenstein and Shaw as they stood on the patio. "Guys, we got a break. Those traffic cams finally paid off. Once we had a track to follow, Hickam Air Field launched two tracking drones." He looked at Shaw. "I guess you were able to pull some strings?"

Shaw smiled and nodded. "Like I said before, you have the unlimited resource."

Walker smiled. "Thanks, it made all the difference. One of the drones found the van and tracked it as it turned south off of Lunalilo Freeway, or Highway 1, onto Ward Ave. Then it took a left on Ala Moana Boulevard followed by a right on Ala Moana Park Drive, to right here where they parked, right here." He showed them an aerial photo.

"This is a row of dilapidated buildings on the north side of the Kewalo Basin. Kewalo Basin used to be pretty active but it is older now; kind of a poor man's mixed-use harbor for commercial fishing and recreational vessels. Not much charter work there but the old loading docks are still available for harbor tenants and guests."

Shaw said, "Tell me about the marina and waterfront area?"

Walker said, "The various buildings, piers and docks were constructed over many decades. Most have been repaired, renovated and/or demolished and replaced since their original construction. HPD has evacuated occupants from any structure close to the scene. There are about 250 boat slips ranging in size but less than half of them occupied. We've already made a call to the marina office. Luckily, today there were only a few folks in the area and we have them moved out."

Phillips said, "Let me get with my team leaders. How long will it take to get there?"

Walker checked his watch. "This time of day probably thirty minutes, but if we wait until rush hour... you're talking an hour to an hour and a half."

*****

Emma emerged from the house and walked to her father. "Anything yet, Dad?"

Shaw turned. "We have an idea of where the kids might be being held. We ain't waiting a second longer than necessary and I'm going to be there when this goes down." Emma nodded and hugged her dad.

Paul kissed her forehead and said, "I'm going home, I will be there with Annie when you call."

"Go, all we can do right now is pray," Emma said.

Chapter Fifteen

Phillips, his two team leaders, Tim Shaw and Walker, were gathered around the front end of Phillips' sedan, leaning over the hood, studying a map. Phillips said, "Okay our first unit will park here, and advance on foot to here..." He pointed out the location on the map before asking his first team leader, "How long to get in position here?"

"On foot, seven minutes, ten at the most."

Phillips nodded. "The second unit will turn South off of H1 on Mccully Street then right on Kapiolani Boulevard across Kalakaua Avenue, left on Atkinson Drive then onto Ala Moana State Regional Park Drive, and plug up the hole from the rear. Medical personnel will be positioned here..."

"Any layout of the building they're in?" Shaw asked.

Phillips flipped a faded blueprint out. "This is old but probably pretty accurate. Single story, wood construction with five rooms. As soon as Team One is in place, they'll scan the building with infrared to locate the people inside. Gentlemen, on the signal we hit them hard and fast, it's the only chance these kids have got. There's a fifty-fifty chance we can get them out unharmed."

Shaw reached down and pulled his .38 from an ankle holster and checked the loads one last time. Next he pulled his 1911 .45, dropped the magazine and pushed on the top round making sure it was full. For the fifth time in five minutes before, he slid the weapon back into his leather shoulder rig. "I'll be with your Team," he said to Team One's leader. "I want you to remember the fifty-fifty-ninety rule: Anytime you have a fifty-fifty chance of getting something right, there's a ninety percent probability you'll get it wrong."

Team One's leader nodded. "Proud to have you, Mr. Shaw, I just ask that you let us do our job without interference."

Shaw said, "I will be focused on the kids. You guys focus on Davis and McAllen; I don't care if they are dead or alive, as long as the kids are okay. We clear?"

"Okay, let's get into position, move out."

"Wait a minute," Shaw said. "What about the water? I don't want these bastards to have a way out."

"I've already sent a team," Walker said. "One of my guys has a small fishing boat; he has four marksmen on it plus three SWAT guys. They are in the harbor already. They won't get away."

Shaw nodded. "Thanks Captain."

"Let's roll out."

Chapter Sixteen

Every nerve ending and muscle fiber in John Rourke's body was on fire, and he still could do nothing. The fire consuming him was total; but slowly... microscopically, the intensity began to diminish. He became more mentally aware but still physically numbed and unable to move. Then, as suddenly as the agony had consumed him, like a switch had been flipped, miraculously it stopped.

Sweat covered his naked skin. Stink from the sweat threatened to smother him, still he could not move. Now, able to focus on the scene around him, it could only be described as... alien. He remembered Arnold, his betrayal... he had glimpses of early moments of semi-clarity. Had he awakened for moments or seconds?

John Thomas Rourke had been captured and now was in the hands of the greatest enemy the planet Earth had ever faced—the Creator. The Creator stepped back in the room, the being's dark grey skin showed a distinct lack of muscular definition.

Rourke assessed the being silently, *Elongated body and a small chest... legs shorter than what one would expect in a human, the humeri and the thighs appeared to the same length as the forearms and shins... no visible sexual characteristics... Head, unusually large in proportion to the body... no hair visible anywhere on the body, including the face... no noticeable outer ears or nose, only small openings or orifices for ears and nostrils... mouth small... opaque black eyes, very large but with no discernible iris or pupil... about four feet tall, maybe slightly more but only by an inch or two...*

It stood for a long time staring at Rourke. The total lack of expression... *disconcerting,* was the only word Rourke could think of. The only movement was the head which periodically moved from side to side; on a human it could have been interpreted as quizzical or thoughtful. Slowly it stepped forward and laid its hand on Rourke's immobilized head; Rourke thought it felt gentle.

Rourke had to clear his throat before he could speak. He tried to say, "Hello, how can I help you?" Only a scratchy squeak came out. Swallowing, Rourke tried again, "Hello, how can I help you." John coughed slightly and pressed on, "I'm sorry but I'm not sure if you understand our language. I would like to communicate with you. I would also appreciate it if you would remove these restraints."

Rourke jiggled his hands and feet to draw attention to the restraints. The creature walked to a panel next to the door and pushed a button; the door opened and as it walked through, it reached back and punched the wall. The restraints opened and the creature moved out of the room as the door shut behind it.

Chapter Seventeen

"Team One in position," the radio squawked. "Infrared shows four body signatures in room one; room two is empty and two body signatures in room three.

"Team Two in position," the radio squawked. "Street blocked and we are set up on the east side of the next building over."

"Sea side is plugged, we're ready when you are." The report came from Walker's team on the fishing boat.

Phillips sat in the mobile command post monitoring the radio and three computer screens. Sweat rolled down his cheeks. The visual feeds came from a drone circling high above, directly overhead, and camera images from two police helicopters that surveyed the neighborhood. The unit's air conditioner hummed ineffectively in the background.

He took a last drag on the cigarette before snubbing it out in the ash tray; he crossed himself, said a silent prayer and keyed the microphone. "Initiate. All operators you have a green light. I say again, initiate. You have a green light."

He leaned back and crossed himself again, wishing he hadn't snubbed out the cigarette.

*****

Team One moved out; half of the team headed for their staging point on the east side of the target building. They were going after the hostage takers. The rest of the team were low crawling through the two foot tall sea grass; fifty feet to go. Crawling from what little concealment the sea grass gave, they made their way to the west wall of the structure.

They prepared to breach the west wall in room one and snatch the hostages.

Agent Dale Roberts stuck the small explosive charges on the west wall, the heavy adhesive pads holding them securely to the old wooden wall, and plugged in the electronic caps. He flipped the cover of the activation switch on the detonator and waited for sounds of a double click in his headphone receiver. Team Two moved down the Ala Moana State Regional Park Drive to cover the target building and snag anyone coming out.

Roberts pushed the blinking red button on the detonator; six small explosions took out the wall and four men rushed inside to grab the hostages as Roberts' carbine covered them from the gap he had just created. Simultaneously, on the other side of the building, the crash of a battering ram splintered the door frame and flashbang grenades blasted the still of the air.

Gunfire erupted.

The first man through the wall gap was Tim Shaw. Shaw rushed into the room with his gun hand outstretched, covering the door. He went to the far side of the room and grabbed Tim by his shirt front. In one motion, he jerked the boy to his feet, bent over and flipped him up on his shoulder. His gun hand never wavered. He watched as Paula and Natalie were pulled up and carried bodily out by two men, and Jack snatched from the ground by the last operator.

Shaw, his gun hand still extended, was the last to rush back through the gap in the wall. He kept running, following the three operators to a safe location. Robert's remained, his carbine focused on the door. On the other side of the building the rapid cacophony of gunfire, screams and shouted commands could be heard. Suddenly it was quiet, except for a shouted single word...

"Clear."

Chapter Eighteen

Almost out of breath, Shaw sat his heavy load down and looked closely at Tim for the first time. "Boy, you're going to have to lose some weight if you're going to keep this up," he said, smiling as he untied the gag. Flipping a four-inch switchblade out, he cut the duct tape around the boy's feet and spun him around to cut the rope from his hands. Then he spun him back to look into Shaw's face. "You okay? You look like hell..."

Tim nodded. "I'm fine, just a little banged up. Thanks Grandpa." Then Tim Rourke pulled away and went to his sister's side. Her bonds and gag had been removed and she stood holding on to the arm of her rescuer. "Sis..." he said. Paula smiled and hugged her brother. Natalie and Jack smiled their relief.

Jack said, "Yeah, Tim. I'm okay too." The cousins laughed and hugged each other. Each of the kids was checked over by medical technicians and EMTs. Their scrapes were cleaned and where necessary, butterfly bandages were added. Stitches would have to wait until they were examined at the hospital ER.

Shaw shook the hands of the other three operators solemnly. "Guys, I owe you one..."

One of them, the tallest smiled. "All in a day's work, Mr. Shaw." Shaw smiled and sat down on the ground and pulling out his cell phone, he dialed Emma. "We got 'em Baby, they're bruised up a little but they're okay. Medics are taking them to Honolulu General, I'll meet you there. I've got to call Paul."

Redialing, Shaw said into the phone, "Paul, they're okay. We have them and they're safe." In the background he could hear Annie crying. "They are transporting the kids to Honolulu General; Emma will meet you there and I'll head up there as soon as everything here is wrapped up. Got to go, we'll talk soon."

He broke the connection without hearing Paul's thanks and called Michael Rourke.

Shaw fumbled in his pocket for a cigarette and his lighter. He could smell the salt water on the breeze; he looked up and watched a single seagull soaring on the air thermals rising from shore. In a slow, tired voice, he said to himself, "I'm getting too old for this..." Taking another drag on the cigarette, he crossed his legs and leaned back on one arm. "Yeah, I'm getting too old for this," he said to the seagull. The smile on his face said otherwise.

Chapter Nineteen

The scene was secure; William Alan Davis and Lee Elwood McAllen lay unconscious on stretchers as the medics worked on them. Davis had taken three rounds; two in the chest and a third had grazed his neck. The chest wounds were serious; the medic said, "I've got him stable but he needs surgery as soon as possible, I think an artery was nicked."

McAllen had fired six shots from his revolver at the operators, none scoring a hit. The operators had returned the favor with more accuracy. McAllen had lost his right thumb; it had been hit when a round blew the little revolver across the room. He took two rounds high on the left side; his medic diagnosed them as "both through and through." McAllen had spun around from the impact; another round had smashed his spinal column.

An EMT said, "Call for the buses, we have to get these two to surgery, STAT! That means, 'sooner than already there.' Let's go!"

Outside a flurry of activity continued; motor cycles, police cars, three ambulances and two fire trucks stood by silently, flashing their emergency lights. Barricades were being set up and the streets would be blocked off for several more hours as the scene of the gun battle was processed.

Phillips, Walker and Shaw stood silently watching. "Kids appear to be okay; Docs at Honolulu General will probably want to keep them overnight for observation just to be on the safe side. The parents are enroute to them now," Walker said.

Phillips said, "No casualties on my side."

"None here either," Walker said. "Pleasure working with both of you."

"Gentlemen it was a good operation," Shaw said. "I speak for the parents and the family when I say you have our undying gratitude. Now if you will excuse me, I'll be at the hospital if you need me. Thank you, thank you again."

Shaw walked to his car and climbing in, turned the ignition; it was over.

*****

Emma, Paul and Annie arrived within seconds of each other. They ran up the ramp leading to the Emergency Room and through the cordon of police officers and EMTS. Paula, Natalie and Jack sat on chairs inside one curtained-off room, watching Tim about to get stitches.

"Man, look at the size of that needle," Jack said, as Tim sat stoically on the edge of the hospital bed. Tim gave him a blazing glance which broke into a wide smile when he saw Emma. "Mom, we're all okay, I promise."

Emma and Annie swarmed toward the kids with Paul a half step behind. Paula and Natalie broke into tears as they hugged their mothers. Paul grabbed Jack up in a bear hug, just as Tim Shaw walked in; he leaned back against the wall and smiled. Paul turned and with Jack, walked over to him.

"Tim," Paul asked, "What can I say? Thank you."

"I'm just glad they're safe. Have you spoken to Michael?"

"Yes, he called right after we left the house to come here. He and Natalia are on their way now to the hospital."

Shaw smiled as he ruffled Jack's hair. "Good," was all he could think to say before he put his arm around his daughter.

Emma looked at him for a long moment and tiptoed to kiss him lightly on the cheek. "Thank you, Dad, thank you so much."

Annie turned around and gave him a big hug, wet tears transferring from her cheek to his. "Tim..." she started but stopped. Shaw wrapped his other arm around her and just stood there, quietly.

Chapter Twenty

"McAllen will be paralyzed from the waist down from now on," the surgeon said as he walked up to Shaw, removing his surgical mask and cap. "The slug in his back... well, we got it out but the damage had already been done. He's down in ICU."

"What about Davis?" Shaw asked.

"Don't know, you can wait on his surgeon, I'm going for a cup of coffee," the doctor said, and walked slowly off. Shaw watched his sweat-soaked back turn the corner. The doors to the other operating suite opened and Davis' surgeon walked out.

"Well?" Shaw asked.

"He'll survive; the EMT was right, one of the slugs nicked an artery. Once we had the bleeder under control, it was pretty much a text book case. We have moved him to ICU, for observation. If we didn't miss something and have to open him up again, you can talk to him in a couple of hours."

Shaw nodded and turned to the police officer next to him. "I want guards outside their doors 24/7 until I say different. Handcuff them both to their beds, and I want an officer inside the rooms with each of them." The officer nodded and walked off speaking into the microphone on his shoulder.

Shaw looked around, everything that needed to be done had been. He glanced at the wall clock above the nurse's station and counted back. "Hmmm," Shaw said to himself. "Seems like this has been going on for a week, time must have stopped. It's only been nineteen hours since this nightmare started." He dug out his lighter and removed the last cigarette from the pack. He crumpled the pack and his empty coffee cup, tossing both in a waste basket as he walked slowly past the elevator. He stopped at the nurse's station, made sure his instructions were understood and walked out of the hospital.

"Damn," he said as he stepped outside. "It's dark already." He lit the cigarette, fumbled for his car keys and walked slowly to the car. With the engine running, he keyed the microphone, gave his call sign and said, "I'm leaving the hospital, I'm heading home. Everything quiet?"

"Affirmative."

"Good, keep it that way. I'm going to bed." Thirty minutes later he parked his car in the street and walked slowly up the drive. Once inside, he walked to his bed, kicking his shoes off on the way. He lay down, still in his clothes, took two deep breaths. He didn't move for the next ten hours.

*****

Evening descended on the quiet streets of Honolulu, the dusk-to-dawn curfew instituted when the disease crisis started, was still in effect. The only sound to be heard was an insistent buzzing. The buzzing of tiny wings; a lot of them.

Chapter Twenty-One

"Mom, the kids are okay," Michael said into the phone the next morning. "Tim Shaw was there when the police rescued them. They're being examined at the hospital as we speak. I've talked to Emma, Paul and Annie and they are okay."

Sarah Rourke-Mann, First Lady of New Germany, breathed a sigh of relief, "Thank God. I'll call Wolfgang and tell him the good news. I'm on the presidential jet and headed your way." Checking the time, she said, "I'll be landing at Honolulu International in less than an hour. I've been waiting on your call; I will see you at the hospital. Any word on your father?"

"No Mom," Michael said. "I'll brief you on that when you get here. I'll have the Secret Service meet you at the airport and they'll bring you to the hospital. I'm glad you're coming, Mom."

Sarah broke the connection and sat unmoving for a moment, *Too much*, she thought. *Too much for me to deal with but, I don't have a choice, do I?* She pulled the information card from the seat pocket and glanced at the information about HI Airport and its next door neighbor, Hickam Air Force Base. Hickam was one of the few remaining totally Air Force controlled facilities in the world. The Japanese bombed Hickam and Pearl Harbor on December 7, 1941.

She knew all of that. *I can't seem to keep my mind focused*, she thought as an inexplicable sense of dread settled on her.

Chapter Twenty-Two

Otto Croenberg stood outside the hospital next to Paul Rubenstein; this time he wore the white jacket of a medical technician and a shortly cut, dark brown wig. A dozen Secret Service agents milled around in plain clothes acting like hospital visitors taking a break. Paul turned to Croenberg. "Otto, I really appreciate you being here. It means a lot."

Croenberg simply shook his hand and with a soft smile said, "Where else would I be, my friend? I'm glad the children are alright."

As three sedans rounded the block, Croenberg flipped his cigarette into the street and said, "I'll see you upstairs, but you won't see me," and turned to go inside.

The three non-descript sedans parked next to the curb and Sarah Mann stepped from the rear passenger compartment of the second, along with two of Wolfgang's security detail; all three vehicles left immediately. The security personnel were in business casual clothes and Sarah was dressed in blue jeans and a pullover with a matching baseball cap and large sun shades. She did not look like the First Lady of New Germany, not at all.

When she saw Paul coming to her, she smiled. Wrapping her in a bear hug, Paul squeezed harder than he meant to, and Sarah let out a 'huff' of breath. Stepping back he said, "I'm sorry Sarah, I didn't mean to squeeze so hard. It's just that seeing you here right now..." He stifled what almost was a whimper.

"Where else would I be, Paul?" She said. "Take me to our darlings, please." Her two-man security detail and six of the Secret Service agents drifted around them as they headed inside. "Security is tight, I see."

Paul nodded. "Precautionary. The bastards who took the kids were captured. Most of this is to ensure your privacy, Sarah. It's not like the old days when we could come and go as we chose. I'm glad this is a 'secret' visit. The fewer people who know you're here the better."

"I know," she said. "Sometimes, I find I actually miss those days... or parts of them anyway." A short ride up the elevator and a short walk down the hall, Sarah stuck her head into a large double room and said, "Well, look who's here."

Calls of "Grandma!" erupted as Paul closed the door behind her. Moments later, Annie came walking up the corridor with cups of coffee. "Your Mom's inside," Paul said. "She just got here."

Annie frowned. "Is she okay? She's been on my mind for the last two hours."

Paul shrugged. "Seems to be... your intuition kicking in again?"

Annie shrugged back. "I don't know, maybe it's just the stress of the kids and what we've all been through." Paul opened the door for her and followed her inside.

Chapter Twenty-Three

Sarah was with Emma; the news of John Rourke's disappearance had stunned her.

Michael and Natalia sat in the living room of the Presidential mansion; their children asleep upstairs. Michael was reading the reports from the Office of Emergency Management; the hantavirus outbreak was reaching critical mass.

Natalia stretched as she stood up from the couch and stepped around the coffee table on which Michael had spread out the half dozen reports. She said, "Michael, I told you I knew the Soviet Union began a bio-weapons program in the 1920s but that during and after the Second World War, Stalin continued to work on his biological weapons."

Michael looked up. "Yes, you told me that."

She nodded. "I know there were several biological research facilities throughout the Soviet Union. Over the years, these were known to have weaponized and stockpiled several bio-agents and pursued basic research on many more. Could they have involvement in this new epidemic?"

"It sure looks that way," he said. "What gets me is the genetic manipulations; did the Russians do research on that?"

She shrugged. "Not much before the Night of the War, but since... I just don't know. What about that extermination plan John was working on before the trip to Mount Rushmore?"

"It begins tomorrow," Michael said, sitting back deeper into the couch cushions; fatigue evident on his face. "National Guard and the Office of Emergency Management are coordinating on the procedures. They seem pretty confident that can wipe out the VBBs. Dr. Kirby is stumped on how they were genetically engineered, but they don't exist it nature. Part Lord Howe Island stick insect, part Rocky Mountain Locust, part scorpion, and they can fly."

"How do we fight them?" She asked.

"Kirby says we're lucky, the original three different species have one thing in common: all three prefer to nest underground in burrows. This new beastie does also. Kirby says that on an individual scale, we can step on them like a cockroach; provided you're wearing heavy shoes or boots."

"But how do we deal with so many?" she asked, her lips turned down in a frown and her brow furrowed with thought.

"With a population density like we're looking at... we have to burn them out," Michael said. "That's what Dad was working on with Lancer. They were modifying regular energy weapons, changing them into flamethrowers. We have enough now to launch the attack on the bugs and Randall Walls thinks he knows where to find them. I just hope he's right."

*****

Fifty National Guardsmen were gathered at the Lancer test range. Six long tables were set up with what looked like eight regular energy weapons laid out on each table, about twenty feet behind each of the firing stations. A hundred yards down range sat a series of targets.

Jim Downey, the primary instructor, picked up one of the black rifles from a table and walked to the firing line. "Good morning, this will be your first class on this weapon. We at Lancer are proud to be a part of this operation." He turned downrange, flipped the activation switch to on and made some small adjustments.

Shouldering the weapon and taking aim, he squeezed the trigger. A stream of green fire erupted in an arch from the muzzle; it traveled down range to impact on a stack of wooden pallets. Intense red/orange flames shot skyward. He placed the weapon on safe before turning to the first group of trainees.

"This started its life as a standard energy rifle," Downey said. "But it wasn't suited to this mission." He pointed to a small device in front of the receiver. "I made this component to correct the problem, it's a frequency modulator. A standard energy weapon sends an individual bolt of high energy downrange; it is modulated plasma, modulated and set at very high range. That setting is necessary for accuracy, almost at a pinpoint level."

"We had to go back and reverse-engineer the 'problem' the original designers had to overcome. In the beginning, they struggled with how to increase the 'flow' of energy to a 'usable projectile' of energy. That was what was so time consuming in the original design; how it functioned. Understand?"

No one seemed to.

"Look," Downey said. "They started with a flow and improved it to a pulse; the opposite of what we need. With this modulator, I reduced those individual bolts, or pulses, of high energy back to a stream of lower energy plasma; lower energy but higher temperature. That means instead of single bolts of high energy, the weapon is capable of generating a continuous stream of energy of high temperature plasma. You don't have the long range accuracy or the impact devastation, but you have blistering heat, approaching 2,000 degrees that can be sprayed like a stream of water."

"That'll melt the barrel, won't it?" one of the National Guard sergeants asked.

"Watch again," Downey said as he aimed and pulled the trigger; the jet of plasma energy leaped from the barrel again. "The flame doesn't start until the stream has already left the barrel by two, two and a half feet. Neither you or the weapon will be exposed to the high temperature."

"So, there's no danger to the operator," the sergeant said.

"Not from the weapon, this is a proven design with proven technology. All we really did..." He thought about a proper analogy. "We didn't change ammo, just how it functions."

"How about the capacity, how long will one weapon function if it starts out fully charged?" another Guardsman asked.

"On continuous stream, probably fifteen minutes. Use short, controlled streams, double... even triple that," Downy said. "It uses the same energy pack currently in use to power the energy rifle. All of you are familiar with the base weapon already. To reload, it just takes a few seconds and you're back at full charge, ready to start over again."

Downy continued, "Once we solved the flow problem, we didn't have to fabricate or recreate a weapon that none of you are familiar with or have any experience with. This design eliminated the bulky, heavy fuel backpack, plus the nozzle and igniter contraption from the old style flamethrower."

"This module only increases the normal weight of the weapon by about three-quarters of an ounce. And we've eliminated the time involved in training people to safely operate this weapon platform. If you can spray a water hose, you can operate this weapon."

Someone from the back of the crowd asked, "What happens if it becomes necessary to switch back to the regular energy rifle? Or, are we going to have to carry both weapons?"

Downey shook his head. "Not at all, all we have to do is remove the modulator and the weapon returns to its normal functioning. That can be done in the field by the operator, without any special tools and only about ten minutes of training. Now, who wants to try it first?"

Thirty minutes later, all of the Guardsmen had fired and qualified on the weapon. The next class of Guardsmen arrived as the first class boarded buses to return to base.

Chapter Twenty-Four

It took Randall Walls hours to lay out the search pattern; in addition to Oahu, there were seven other main islands. Hawaii, Maui, Kahoolawe, Lanai, Molokai, Kauai and Niihau and over a 150 separate islands in the Hawaiian chain. The total came to almost 6,500 square miles, not including uninhabited islets, rocks, coral reefs, and atolls.

On Oahu alone, he had activated almost thirty local agencies in response to such an outbreak; the Capital City Fire and Police Departments, County Sheriff's Offices and School Districts, County Health Departments, Air Quality, and Emergency Management to mention a few. Add to that mix the Red Cross, pharmacies, medical examiners, hospitals, and the rest; it added up pretty quickly.

*****

Days earlier, General Sullivan, the Chief of Staff, had asked General Rodney Thorne if he thought he could fly the captured UFO. Thorne had said he could, but one of the super brains is going to "have to tell me how to turn the damn thing on and take off. Frankly, I don't have a clue."

That evening, after much thought, Thorne still didn't have a clue but he did have a hunch. He drove back to the hanger, flashed his ID to the guard and saw Dr. Dalton, the Senior Flight Surgeon, bent over a table studying files. Thorne climbed the steps that led to the UFO's hatch, sat down in the pilot's seat, thinking, *Okay, let's see if this works.*

Swiveling the seat around, he sat there looking at the blank control panel. "Feels right," he said aloud. "Feels right." When he reached out with his left hand and laid it on the surface of the panel, nothing happened. He moved his right hand and laid it on the surface; still nothing. He pulled them back and sat there for a moment, thinking. Then he had laid both hands at the same time on the panel and thought, *On.*

Right in front of him a holographic image sprang into view, he had jerked back in surprise. The image vanished. "Whoa, I didn't expect that," he said, wiping his hands on his pants' leg. He did it again and the image returned; this time he left his hands in place. He thought, *Systems,* and data began to stream across the hologram. *That's good, it is in English.* The order of the data was different from what he was used to but it was all there. Taking a deep breath, he thought, *Remain on standby.*

He went to the hatch and hollered for Dalton, "Doc, have you got a camera?"

"In my office."

Thorne ordered, "Get it and come in here, hurry. Make sure the camera has good batteries and a new memory card." Less than ten minutes later Dalton returned with the camera, slightly out of breath. Thorne sat back down and said, "Get the camera ready and watch this." Placing his hands again on the panel he thought, *Resume.* The holographic image sprang into being.

"Holy crap," Dalton exclaimed. "How did you do that?"

"See if it registers on the camera," was all Thorne said.

"Yeah, it does."

"Then start taking pictures, damn it. Don't use the flash." For the next thirty minutes, Thorne ran through the program, Dalton snapped pictures until Thorne thought he had seen it all. Finally Thorne thought, *Off.* The image faded and he swiveled the pilot seat around. Sweat glistened across his forehead as he said, "Whew, did it work?"

Dalton reviewed the images and nodded. "How did you figure it out?"

Thorne wiped his face and smiled. "I kept thinking about what you said the other day, 'It was as if the pilot had to wear' the craft to fly it. I couldn't shake the idea but I couldn't see each craft being designed for individual pilots. It had to be simpler than that. Flying is flying... we were over thinking the way to do it; I just simplified the thinking process."

The next day, Thorne and Dalton briefed the Chief of Staff, General Sullivan, on their progress. Sullivan said, "I have to get back to headquarters. I will expect a full briefing from you tomorrow.'"

The next day, after Dalton had left the briefing, Sullivan told Thorne, "We don't have anything in our arsenal that has its flight or weapons capabilities. One ship may not be enough to stop an invasion, but it could be a hell of a surprise for the invaders. It could buy us a little time."

Since that day, Thorne had spent hours in the cockpit of the "flying egg." Using the visual display, he was able to locate the cloaking system and the weapons system. He was now comfortable that he could fly it. Sullivan insisted, "In everyone's view, we have to keep any flights secret."

"Though difficult to detect cloaked, it was detected. Through more luck than skill, Randall Walls and Paul Rubenstein did it. They realized the 'patterns' were flight paths of unknown and cloaked air craft. That discovery led to the Battle at the Forest where Rubenstein almost died."

*****

The first flight had gone reasonably well; the hardest part for Thorne had been learning to keep both hands in position on the control panel.

He was used to a stick in one hand, thrust control in the other and controlling directional maneuvering with his feet. Thorne had to sit relatively still and control the flight with his thoughts. It had taken time "getting used" to the change.

Once, he had unconsciously moved his hands and lost control of the craft. That sent him spiraling downward almost 3,000 thousand feet before he regained control. After the flight, he had told the General, "It would almost be easier to have someone who's never flown to learn this craft. I have to unlearn just about everything I have been doing all these years."

"Yes," the General had agreed. "But once you get the 'hang' of this thing, your combat experience will be invaluable. A computer geek used to playing combat games would have an easier time in the beginning but they wouldn't know what to do when the shit hits the fan."

Thorne and Dr. Dalton had come up with what they hoped would be a fix. They would superglue Velcro straps onto the control panel for Thorne's hands. They felt those straps would provide a physical reminder for Thorne to "keep your hands were they're supposed to be."

Today, they would find out if it would work; it was time for the second cloaked flight of the alien craft.

Chapter Twenty-Five

The list of equipment John Rourke had asked Paul to retrieve from the Retreat before the Mount Rushmore operation had been lengthy. Except for a few... a very few private collectors—technological equipment from the mid twentieth century did not exist. Even at Mid-Wake, the obsolete equipment had long ago been discarded in favor of changing technology. There simply had been no room in the confines of Mid-Wake for non-essentials.

When Paul and his "crew"—John Michael, Timothy and John Paul—returned from the Retreat, they brought back old style computers; some that operated on the old floppy discs, others that processed punch cards, old operating systems that covered a wide variety of out of date systems and even old wire recorders. After all, the unknown data and artifacts from the Hall of Records potentially were stored on technology that simply no longer existed.

Rourke's fear was they might be able to retrieve it but, depending on how it was stored, might not be able to decipher the data.

Paul had given the "haul" to Jose Zima and his computer nerds. They were to get the equipment functional and start the recovery of data. Zima and his crew had worked for days cleaning and refurbishing the mechanical components.

"Luckily," Zima had told Paul after he examined the equipment, "From what I can see, the storage conditions at John's Retreat seem to have been ideal. I don't see anything that causes me concern. We'll have a few components I'm sure that we may have to fabricate, but mostly just a good cleaning and this stuff should work as well as it ever did. It is amazing that in today's world we have to rely on technology over a half millennium old to find out information."

The Hall of Records data was examined; some of the information had been lost. The old style paper that had been used for printed materials had suffered badly. The porcelain plates, floppy discs and electronically recorded data were in the best shape; particularly those dictated onto the wire recorder system.

Zima told the President's representative for Cultural Conservation, Dr. Adam Levine, "Wire recorders date back to the late 1890s. They were used for dictation and telephone recording and were made for many decades. The brief heyday of wire recording was from 1946 to 1954, particularly by the government. There were some home entertainment applications, but that did not last very long. While phonograph records could accommodate only a few minutes of audio on each side of a vinyl disc, the steel wire could be repeatedly re-recorded and allowed much longer recordings to be made."

"The wire was also a much more compact storage medium than magnetic tape. They were used in aircraft cockpit voice recorders and flight data recorders in the early 1940s. The steel wire was compact, robust and more heat-resistant than plastic-based magnetic tape, and wire recorders were used to record data in satellites and other unmanned spacecraft, from the 1950s to the 1970s. The heavy-duty recorders used large spools and could record hours of conference or meeting minutes. This is where the majority of 'relevant' material in our search was found."

Levine asked, "So, of this 'relevant' material, what did you recover?"

Zima smiled. "Something called The Stargate Project. This was the code name for a Defense Intelligence Agency program to investigate claims of psychic phenomena with potential military and domestic application. The information gleaned was vague, included irrelevant and erroneous data, and there was reason to suspect that its project managers had changed the reports. Remember, information on psychic research in foreign countries was sketchy and poorly detailed. Mostly rumors from second-hand sources and unreliable disinformation sources from the Soviet Union. I really think it was a cover story."

"What do you mean?" Levine asked.

"The best way to keep a secret is to hide it in the open. The Hall of Records' material that the CIA and DIA used, documents the insight and technology obtained during the alien contacts of the late forties, through the mid-fifties and beyond. The cover story was that U.S. intelligence sources believed the Soviet Union was spending sixty million rubles annually on 'psychotronic' research. The truth is that was 'shared technology' obtained from the aliens."

"What the hell is 'psychotronic' research?" Levine asked.

"A set of protocols designed for the research of clairvoyance and out-of-body experiences and a host of other paranormal abilities; we found a lot of data on telepathy for example. Then after spending millions of dollars, Stargate was shut down and the studies either secreted or discredited by evaluators."

"Apparently, the aliens withheld some details," Zima continued. "In any event, neither the Russians nor our government had much success with psychotronics."

Chapter Twenty-Six

Dr. Eric Stevens, the County Medical Examiner, had been the first to diagnosis the new virus. Even then, the outbreak of the disease had gone on unchecked. Temporary emergency facilities were springing up all over the state; so far to no avail. The body count was continuing to rise and new outbreaks were being reported daily.

Stevens called for a conference with the Director of the Center for Disease Control, Dr. William Barlow. Barlow looked tired and haggard. Normally well-groomed and neat in appearance, Barlow looked like he had not shaved in days or slept in nights. Stevens asked, "Bill, has there been any progress at all? This outbreak is tasking the military and medical communities to the breaking point. We are knocking on the door of a pandemic. We need answers."

Barlow rubbed his face with both hands, his exhaustion evident. "Eric, we have been experimenting, looking for some way... any way, to develop a cure for this new strain of hantavirus or a vaccine. Nothing has worked so far, but last evening one of my people suggested a possible approach. We're working it right now."

"What is it?" asked Stevens.

Barlow smiled. "Mistletoe."

"Mistletoe? I thought all that was good for is a kiss around Christmas."

Barlow explained, "From the Druids to the present, mistletoe has played a role in traditional medicine as a remedy for headaches and seizures; long considered a natural healer. Today the leaves, shoots and berries of the Mistletoe plant are well known sources of various compounds with cancer-fighting activity. Four categories of compounds are used as cancer therapies, including alkaloids, polysaccharides, lectins and viscotoxins. He thinks it might be part of the answer."

"He is focused on one of these species, Korthalsella. They have enlarged stems and reduced leaves, look like an aerial cacti. While all species have had a range of drugs developed from them, viscum album seems the best from studies. One extract appears to work by enhancing activity of the immune system, which improves quality of life, and reduces fatigue, nausea, vomiting and depression.

"My guy thinks we might be able to make something that would work on the modified hantavirus."

*****

Thorne fastened the buckles of his seat harness; out of habit, reached down to the zippered pocket on the leg of his Nomex flight suit and pulled out his leather-palmed pilot's gloves. The flameproof Nomex fabric would protect his hands, while the leather gave him grip and traction on the controls. Smirking to himself, *Problem is, there aren't any controls.* He refolded the gloves and put them back in the leg pocket. He laid his left hand on the control pad and secured his wrist with the Velcro strap. Looking up he said, "Your turn, Doc."

The Senior Flight Surgeon, Dr. Dalton, cinched up the strap securing the right arm. "You ready, General?"

Thorne shrugged his shoulders. "Hell if I know, Doc. I think so... Only one way to find out... take this thing up and see."

"You sure you don't want this?" Dalton said, holding up a parachute.

"No, wouldn't do any good anyway. If something goes seriously wrong, I won't have time to get out of this thing. Besides, there's no room in the seat for it. Guess I just better not screw up."

"Okay, you forgot your Comm unit, I'll buckle it on your head and get out," Dalton said. "You don't have to push any buttons or switches, just talk. We'll be recording everything you say, just in case..."

"Yeah," Thorne said, "just in case you need another pilot. Thanks Doc, see ya when I see ya... If I see ya."

Dalton waved and Thorne could hear the hiss as the hatch closed. He cleared his throat and settled down to business. "Research Craft 1, Comm check."

"Comm check, roger, Research 1. We read you 5 x 5."

"Roger, Research 1. I read you 5x5 also, requesting permission to launch."

"Roger, Research 1. You have permission, good luck."

Thorne positioned his hands on the control pad and thought, *Systems on.* The holographic image sprang to life. *Ship integrity check,* it showed sealed. *Power on, cloak on.* There was an almost indiscernible whine as the ship powered itself up. *Launch sequence activate, go to cruising speed 450, altitude 20,000 feet.*

The silver, egg-shaped vehicle sprang into the air, climbing quickly. *So far so good,* Thorne thought. Aloud he said, "Okay you alien bucket of bolts, let's see what you can do."

Chapter Twenty-Seven

Days before, Manfred Schmidt, the head of security for New Germany's President, Wolfgang Mann, had entered the Presidential Office. "Good evening Mr. President. Is there word on the situation in Hawaii yet?"

Mann smiled. "Yes, Herr Schmidt. I just spoke to my wife; the children have been rescued and are all fine." Checking his watch Mann said, "The First Lady will be landing there shortly and should be with the children and their families in less than an hour."

Schmidt smiled. "I am truly pleased, Sir. I know that lifts a heavy burden from both of you. I agree, I think it was wise to make her trip a secret."

"Yes, no need for a big show, just a mother and grandmother seeing her family. As far as everyone here knows, my wife has the flu and is on bed rest in the Executive Mansion." Mann smiled and pointed at a chair in front of his desk. "You asked for a meeting Herr Schmidt; what can I do for you? Would you care for some coffee?"

Schmidt said as he shook his head, "No, thank you, Sir." He opened his briefcase and pulled a file, opened it and laid it on Mann's desk. "Sir, I'm afraid we may have a problem."

Mann perused the file quickly and said, "You mean we're not finished with these vermin yet?"

"It appears we are not, Sir. The brother of the one Herr Generaloberst Rourke referred to in his report as 'Woody the Woodpecker,' was actually named Johann Burkholter. He's the younger brother of Horst Burkholter, a lieutenant in the more militant arm of the Neo-Nazi movement, and it seems he wants revenge for his brother's death."

Wolf frowned. "Do you believe there is an involvement in what just occurred in Hawaii?"

"No Sir," Schmidt shook his head. "They do not appear to have that type of capability. They are more home grown in their activities. We believe they may be targeting you and the First Lady, however."

"Do you have any idea how they would target us?"

Schmidt sighed. "Frankly Sir, no... no we don't. After Burkholter's brother was killed by Herr Generaloberst Rourke, everything seemed to go quiet. It has only been in the past few days we noticed chatter starting back up. Burkholter, the older brother, had been active in the Democratic German Republic and we believe he was instrumental in the removal and subsequent assassination of President Croenberg."

Mann merely nodded but thought to himself, *Excellent, then it is still perceived that Croenberg was assassinated. I am sure that Paul Rubenstein will be glad to hear this.* Michael had briefed his stepfather on Croenberg's resurfacing. "That I find very interesting, Helmut. For your information, we still don't have an idea of when the First Lady will return to New Germany. With the kidnapping of our grandchildren and another family emergency... she may be gone for some time."

"Honestly Sir, I find that to our advantage. The threat seems to be localized, that means the primary targeting would, of necessity, be limited to you," Schmidt said. "We are revamping some of your travel and speaking itinerary but frankly... we just aren't that concerned."

Mann smiled. "Good, I am glad to hear that. Thank you, Helmut, keep me posted." Schmidt stood, shook hands with his President and left the office.

*****

"Michael," Mann said into the phone. "I understand your extermination operation is set to begin tomorrow. Is that accurate?"

"That's right," Michael said. "I wanted to check with you... have you seen an outbreak there yet?"

"No, thank God," Mann said. "It looks like only your country was targeted. However, it is possible that the carriers simply have not arrived here... yet. I'm hoping your operation will be successful. In the event the bugs show up here, I want to have a plan in place to reduce their impact."

"Totally understand, Wolfgang," Michael said. "We got caught in the surprise, we weren't ready, and we have already had substantial loss of life."

"Any word on John? Your mother and I are both concerned."

"No," and in that single word, Wolfgang Mann could hear the anger and frustration of his stepson. "No word, no contact, no ransom demands. All I know is he seemingly vanished off the face of the earth during the evacuation from Mount Rushmore."

Mann was silent for a long moment. "Michael, you know better than anyone that your father is a survivor. As long as we don't have a body or conformation of his death, we have to believe he is alive. And if John Rourke lives, he'll find a way to get back to us all."

Michael was silent, finally he said, "If, is an awfully big word to just have two letters."

Chapter Twenty-Eight

Otto Croenberg sat in the suite he had at Honolulu's largest and most opulent hotel. He handed a cup of black coffee to Rubenstein and said, "I'm glad to learn the children are safe and sorry to hear about Dr. Rourke, my friend. How is rest of the family dealing with it?"

"As well as can be expected," Paul said. "Sarah is staying with Emma to help her with the baby. It is a lucky thing they get along." Paul sipped his coffee and asked, "What have you got for me, Otto?"

Croenberg nodded. "Please give my salutations to the family and particularly to Sarah. I've conversed with the new Mrs. Rourke but I only met Sarah that once, long ago on the ship. Paladin was its name, was it not?"

Paul nodded.

Otto said, "Anyway, I found Sarah to be an especially intriguing woman, give her my best. Now, as you know, the Neo-Nazism movement began after World War II as social and political movements seeking to revive the far-right-wing tenets of Nazism. The term Neo-Nazism can also refer to the ideology of these movements. In short order, it became a global phenomenon, with organized representation in many countries, as well as international networks.

"In some European and Latin American countries, laws were enacted that prohibit the expression of pro-Nazi, racist, anti-Semitic or homophobic views. Many Nazi-related symbols are banned in European countries in an effort to curtail Neo-Nazism."

"But," Paul said. "Nothing... none of those legal actions slowed the Neo-Nazi movement."

Otto nodded. "Correct, it grew throughout Europe. In Russia, Neo-Nazis openly admired Adolf Hitler and used the German Nazi swastika as their symbol. Russian Neo-Nazis were characterized by racism, anti-Semitism, homophobia and extreme xenophobia towards people from Asia.

"Russian Neo-Nazis wanted to take over the country by force, and put serious effort into preparing for this. Switzerland, Mongolia, Costa Rica, Burma and even the United States were touched by the movement."

"Then came the Night of the War," Paul said. "Even that did little to stop the movement."

"No," Otto said. "Nothing did and I'm convinced that the threat from them is real, again. I saw their influence in my old country and I believe they have expanded their goals."

"To what end?" Paul asked with concern.

"The 'end' is simple: world domination, that goal has never changed. Where? Everywhere."

Paul shook his head. "Once, I think I was in the fifth grade, a woman who suffered the holocaust came to talk to my class. Her name was Mrs. Van Thyn. She told us of the camps and showed us the tattoo on her left arm. It had become almost unreadable but she knew what it said. She had to yell it out for twelve months during the morning lineups at the Nazi-run death camp, the last time shortly before the U.S. Army arrived, liberating the camp."

"She told us, 'Physically surviving was the easier part. What's important is that you do not go insane. That's the part you can work on. I kept repeating: I will survive, I will survive. I was nineteen when my parents, two aunts, an uncle and I were forced from our homes and loaded on a cargo train.'

"When they arrived at the camp, the camp doctor separated her from her family; she never saw them again.

"When the Army arrived, they fed the survivors slowly because too much food, they explained, would kill them. But she said she couldn't resist and ate 'day and night.' When weighed the first time, she weighed just seventy-three pounds but reached ninety-five pounds three weeks later, when she hopped on the roof of a train for the long journey home. She hoped to find a surviving relative waiting for her, but all had perished."

Chapter Twenty-Nine

"I want our President and his bitch wife dead," Horst Burkholter said, slamming his fist on the table. "It was Wolfgang Mann that allowed John Rourke in to rescue his wife. My brother died on that mission, killed by Rourke. My brother just wanted to ransom Mann's wife; that would have financed our operations for years. Rourke killed him."

"I know, Horst," said Peter Vale.

Helmut Freed said, "And my brother Franz sits in prison with no hope for release."

"I've read the reports. He is the one John Rourke referred to as 'Pocked Mark' and I believe he is two years older than you," Vale said.

"Correct, Rourke's slug permanently crippled Franz's right arm which now hangs useless by his side. I want not only the New German President and First Lady, but Rourke as well."

"My sources," Vale said, "say Rourke is off on a mission above the glacial line in North America. We will have to settle for what we can get now and hope to settle our debts with the others later."

"Rourke can wait," Burkholter said with a sneer. "First, I want him to suffer the loss of his friend and ex-wife. When his time comes, the debt will be paid in full. Now," he said, "when do we kill President Mann and his wife, Sarah?"

Vale nodded. "The First Lady has not been seen for several days and supposedly, she is sick. If that is the case, to take them both out it will probably be necessary to attack them at the Presidential residence. That appears the best way to be sure we can kill both. However, the President has a speaking engagement in two days; if his wife is present, we will kill them both there. If she is not, we will move on the Presidential residence when he returns."

Burkholter asked, "So how do we pull that off? Those two locations will both have tremendous security."

Vale smiled. "Let's take a ride gentlemen."

*****

Four hours later, they pulled into an abandoned mine in the forest east of the capital city.

"Okay," Burkholter said. "What's your surprise, what's the answer? How do we kill them?"

Vale indicated a road on the far side of the mine. "Put these on and watch." He handed each a set of ear protectors, placing a set over his own ears. Keying a handheld radio, he said simply, "Begin."

A plain white cargo truck charged out of the jungle and down the road. Suddenly, doors opened on both sides of the cargo hold, and a second later, a barrage of missiles came streaking out of the vehicle headed for a concrete block house that had served as the mine's headquarters. Following the circular road, the truck emptied its load of rockets and belched machine gunfire. An instant later, the demonstration was over.

"Holy Crap," Freed said, as he removed the ear protection.

Vale smiled. "Yes, indeed. My contacts were able to obtain rocket launch pods from seven helicopters that were retired from active duty with the Democratic Republic of Germany. These have been donated to your cause."

"Why?" Freed said.

"Let us just say that my government's goals and your own goals have aligned for the moment. It is your desire to rid the world of Wolfgang Mann and his wife and theirs as well; albeit for different reasons.

With Mann's government destroyed, the Democratic Republic of Germany believes they can consolidate power between the two countries and take more control of world events."

"You said you have seven pods, we have seen only one," Burkholter said.

"Six vehicles to match this one are waiting for you in the capital city. The rocket pods can be triggered by the driver who will be able, within a few degrees, to adjust their trajectory. Whichever location we settle on for the attack, the logistics are the same. Each vehicle will need a driver and a machine gunner to wreak havoc and assist in the getaway. Now, do you have ten other competent and dedicated helpers that can assist?"

Chapter Thirty

There had been final pressure checks to ensure the integrity of the UFO's hull was still intact. As no ejection system had been integrated into the craft, it was deemed unnecessary as was the parachute Thorne had left behind. "If something happens, I will be focused on saving the craft and me. I could never get outta the hatch in time," he explained to Dr. Dalton.

After thirty minutes of normal flight acrobatics, during which Thorne had maintained contact with the flight control panel, he was ready. Speed trials came next and he climbed to 47,000 feet to ensure he was above all military and civilian traffic, then opened the craft up to three-quarters speed. A commercial airliner would have taken between seven to eight hours, depending on head winds, to make the flight from Honolulu to the devastated coastline where Reno, Nevada, had once stood. Now the city was called Port Reno. He made it in less than an hour.

"Research 1 to tower."

"Go ahead, Research 1."

"Research 1, control and speed checks completed. You guys have all of the telemetry I presume."

"Roger, Research 1. You are cleared for the next phase."

"Roger, Research 1 climbing."

Thorne increased speed by twenty-five percent and set the vehicle on a new course and heading…up. Seconds later, the last of the haze from Earth's atmosphere faded and the inky black of space swallowed the ship. With the sun behind him, the only light came from stars, now no longer filtered by the atmosphere, the stars no longer blinked. Watching the view screen, Thorne said simply, "Oh my God."

He had launched into space, the first man to do so in almost seven hundred years.

Chapter Thirty-One

Zima was tired, and his team wasn't in any better shape. Michael Rourke watched the view screen on the telecomm. "Jose, when was the last time you and your people really slept?"

Zima looked up then glanced at his watch and made a calculation. "Not sure, close to thirty-six hours I'd guess."

Michael shook his head and said, "Thanks for the effort; what can you tell us?"

Zima wiped his face with both hands before answering, "Mr. President, this has been a very intense time. First of all, I hate to say not all of the material retrieved from the Hall of Records was saved. Frankly, we're not even sure yet what was lost. The specific information you were tasking us with was saved, but I need some time to prepare a briefing for you on the findings."

"I need it as soon as you can, Jose."

"I understand, Mr. President, but I need a few more hours at least."

Michael checked his watch; it was already almost 11:00 P.M. "Okay, Jose... let's do this. Let's set up for nine o'clock in the morning. That will give you and your people time to finish and get a little shut-eye." With a smile, Michael added, "Don't want you dozing off while you're briefing us."

Zima nodded. "Thanks Mr. President, it is appreciated. See you at 0900."

*****

Zima looked a little better, but not much, when Michael saw his face on the screen. "Morning, Mr. President. Are you ready?"

"Yes, Jose," Michael said.

Zima turned to one of his technicians. "Leonard, are you ready for the first display?" Off screen, a man nodded and flipped a switch. A single document sprang into view on the wide screen. Zima said, "Sir, this is incontrovertible proof that long ago, centuries in fact, contact with the aliens was established, and my concern is this paints a significantly different view of them than what we have currently."

"What do you mean?" Michael asked.

"Those initial contacts appear not only peaceful but productive," Zima said. "It appears to us that our current view of the aliens is not at all in alignment with those earlier contacts."

"Based on what?"

"Luckily, we salvaged a lot from Rushmore. Let me give you a quick overview then we can drill down on specifics. We recovered volumes of information concerning the contacts as far back as the late 1800s and into the 1940s, 50s and 60s," Zima said. "We have transcribed a lot of this information but I think you need to listen to the people involved in those early contacts and what they recorded at the time, in their own words. Leonard, are you ready with the sound track?"

Again, Leonard nodded and flipped another switch; scratchy noise came from the computer but soon settled into a very well-modulated recording. Michael listened for several minutes before saying, "Then it is true."

Jose Zima looked at Michael. "Sir, we were correct in most of our thoughts. There was a conspiracy of hiding the truth that goes back several administrations for several governments across the ancient globe. They included America, Germany, England, Russia and the Chinese. The whole concept of 'coming clean' and announcing contact with an alien race was scrapped and, from that time forward, kept from the public. When war finally came, most records—even entire facilities—disappeared and were replaced with half-truths, down-right lies and conspiracy theories. That is where everything was left—until now; and frankly, the veil of secrecy has been obliterated.

"We found the copy of the original report concerning the alien contact with the German government in 1933. The story of it, having been smuggled out of pre-war Germany by one of our operatives, was true. We also found the original, never declassified report on the Roswell incident and photographs of 'artifacts' from the crash. Now here's the kicker. We found a copy of the formal agreement between an alien race and the U.S. Government held at Holliman Air Force Base in 1954.

"The terms of this agreement allow for an exchange of anti-gravity technology, new metals, alloys, and environmental technologies to assist the earth with free energy and medical application regarding the human body. In exchange the aliens were allowed to study human development, both in the emotional and consciousness makeup, and to reside here on earth. In addition to that document, there were copies of the original exchange material. These had been moved from the Blue Moon NSA facility to the Hall of Records around the Night of the War, to protect them.

"It was a good thing Rourke kept those old microform machines. We were able to read both the film and paper versions and they contained micro reproductions of a great many documents. Most not relevant to this subject, but even those have been invaluable in documenting some gaps in our historical knowledge. Those images were reduced to about one twenty-fifth of the original document size, or smaller.

"There were reels of microfilm, aperture cards and the flat sheets used for microfiche, and some of the old micro cards. Those were similar to microfiche, but printed on cardboard rather than photographic film. In any event, we were able to read the information, thanks to you having examples of that old technology.

"The wire recorders, especially the Protona's Minifon miniature recorder, gave us a tremendous amount of information. While we lost some sound quality due to the nearly hair-thin wire, it had the advantage in that it was a much more compact storage medium than tape. Most of the old magnetic tape recordings degraded beyond recovery. Almost all of that information is lost forever. Frankly, it wasn't a surprise, but we were hoping they would have lasted.

"Here's the big find... the President's Book of Secrets. We have it; actually, we have them. There were several volumes ranging from the first. Velum was used for all of them. Each volume contains the private thoughts of between five to eight of the presidents, depending on world events and how verbose a particular president was. It is no longer just an urban legend.

"We confirm alien contact was made; no question about that any longer. Unfortunately, we can also confirm that the human race is in breach of contract."

Michael frowned. "What are you talking about... a breach of contract?"

"Yes Sir... a breach of contract. As I'm sure you know a breach of contract occurs when a legally binding agreement, or bargained-for exchange, is not honored by one or more of the parties to the contract. This can be for non-performance or interference with the other party's performance. If the party does not fulfill his contractual promise, or has given information to the other party that he will not perform his duty as mentioned in the contract, or if by his action and conduct he seems to be unable to perform the contract, he is said to breach the contract."

"And the human race had a contract with the aliens?"

"Yes Sir, several."

Chapter Thirty-Two

New Germany's executive mansion is called Bellevue. It is a three story, three-winged, classic modern building occupying not less than fifty thousand square feet. Located in the capital city of New Brandenburg, it sits on a twelve-acre plot of land circled by a traffic "roundabout" common in the older cities of Europe. Six streets converge and circle the residence.

The main section faces north and holds the Presidential office, several conference rooms, the communications room, and offices for the Chief of Staff, Presidential Security and the Press Secretary. The East Wing serves as office space for the President's Press Room, a multitude of secondary officials such as the Presidential Security Team, Transportation Director and various others, and a small kitchen/cafeteria for workers. It is small, only as compared to the main kitchen.

The West Wing holds the Presidential residence, the main kitchen, a state dining room and a variety of other state functionary rooms, including several for the kitchen and serving staff. One hundred feet beneath Bellevue is the War Room and the emergency Presidential Bunker accessible by a high-speed elevator with a security system.

Horst Burkholter and Helmut Freed had spent three weeks developing two assault plans. Should Plan A—hitting the President and First Lady at the speaking engagement—not be practical for whatever reason, Plan B was to assault Bellevue upon their return.

It was a simple plan. "Simple is always better," Freed had said, numerous times. "The hit will be devastating, multidirectional and the getaway routes simple." Six nondescript cargo vans, of different color and signage, were prepositioned near the Government Building six blocks away. Within each was a driver who would trigger a rocket pod launcher that held nine 2.75 inch rockets, mounted to fire out a side door, and a .762 machine gun mounted on a tripod operated by a second shooter.

The machine gunner would open access doors on both sides of the cargo section just before the attack, to allow back blast from the rockets to escape. The cargo hold was only about fourteen inches wider than the rocket pod. The distance from the traffic lane to the buildings, in both cases, was well within the three-thousand foot accuracy range for the rockets.

Vale had said, "Each pod is loaded with high explosive rounds that will be fired first, followed by anti-personnel rounds that will unleash a hail of shrapnel in the form of both steel ball bearings and fléchettes. The ball bearings will tear through people, and the effect will be double should they impact hard surfaces and rebound. The fléchettes are hundreds of small metal needles with flattened stabilizing fins. They will shred human flesh like a chainsaw. The remaining rockets are incendiary; they'll create a flaming inferno inside the shattered structure."

Vale added, "The devastation from so many rockets hitting either building, coupled with a fusillade of shrapnel and .762 rounds to enhance the confusion and terror as we make our escape, might be considered overkill."

Burkholter smiled. "But that is the plan. I want total overkill and absolute revenge."

The attack had been practiced and simulated numerous times, the only question that remained is would the attack be on the Government Building or Bellevue?

Chapter Thirty-Three

Michael Rourke and Tim Shaw walked slowly up the pathway to Paul Rubenstein's home. When he answered the door, Paul was surprised that the normal entourage of agents had not accompanied the President. "Good morning, Paul," Michael said. "Can you step outside for a minute? We need to talk... privately." The three men walked back to Shaw's sedan and climbed in. Michael turned around from the passenger seat and looked at Paul. "The kids okay?"

Paul nodded. "It was a long night but yes. They vacillate between stony silence and rapid fire retelling us what happened."

"Pretty much the same thing went on at Emma's," Shaw said.

"We haven't talked this morning, how is she doing?" Paul asked.

"That's why we're here, Paul," Michael said, handing a sheet of paper to Paul. "I need you to see her and let her know about this."

Quickly Paul scanned the report; he pushed his wire framed glasses up on his nose then turned to look out the window. "So, this has been confirmed, Michael? Has it been released to the media?"

Rourke nodded. "Yes, it is confirmed, but no, it has not been released and won't be until we find out more. I have everyone on this but right now, this is family business. With your permission, I need to let Annie know. I'm asking you to do the same with Emma."

"Why are we just learning about this?"

Shaw said, "I recommended this plan to Michael, Paul. With the kidnapping I felt there was enough pressure on all of you. Second, there was and is nothing any of the family can do right now about John. If you're going to blame anyone, be mad at me."

Paul nodded. "That makes sense but what do we do about it now?"

Michael spoke up, "We have all of our resources pouring through the satellite feeds from Mount Rushmore trying to find out what happened and where Dad might be. Will you do what I'm asking?"

"Yes," Paul said. "But I want to be there when you tell Annie; she's your sister but she's my wife."

Shaw looked at Michael. "Agreed, then you and I will tell Emma?"

"Yes, does Sarah know?"

Michael shook his head.

After talking to Annie, Michael called for his security detail parked a couple of blocks away, and returned to the Capitol. Paul, Annie and Shaw bundled the kids up and drove to Emma's. An hour and a half later, Rubenstein sat alone on the patio of John Rourke's home. It had gone as expected; not well.

No sooner had her children been saved... to find out her husband was missing... and she might be a widow. No, not well at all.

Annie took all of the children back to her home. Tim Shaw was sitting on the couch, his arm wrapped around Emma's shoulder. Emma... Emma just sat, staring.

Sitting alone on the patio, Paul could have heard the waves breaking on shore; had he been listening. He wasn't. He was lost in memories... memories that begin over six centuries ago with the crash of an airliner and his first meeting with John Thomas Rourke. Ever since, he had followed Rourke through danger after danger, trial after trail... *And now he was gone? Dead?*

Paul pushed his wire framed glasses back in place on his nose. *It can't be true, he can't be gone,* he thought. But it was true. Pulling his phone, Paul dialed Randall Walls' number... "We need to talk, right now. I'll pick you up in thirty minutes." Maybe, just maybe the "patterns" he and Walls had been monitoring during the operation at Rushmore... maybe they could help.

*****

Doctors at all of the medical centers were growing more and more concerned. The outbreak of the genetically modified hantavirus was spreading. The early symptoms included fatigue, fever, and muscle aches, especially in the large muscle groups... thighs, hips, back, and sometimes shoulders. Complaints of headaches, dizziness, chills, and abdominal problems, such as nausea, vomiting, diarrhea, and abdominal pain coupled with coughing and shortness of breath, had packed the emergency rooms.

Where the original hantavirus had a mortality rate of thirty-nine percent, this one was higher, much higher. It was more virulent and aggressive, with symptoms starting in as little as a few hours after exposure and death seemed to follow in twenty-four to thirty-six hours. Hospital morgues had filled up in two days. Emergency morgues were established soon after that. The problem was no longer new patients reporting at a higher level than anyone expected; body disposal was now critical.

Chapter Thirty-Four

Paul had barely entered when his cell phone chirped.

"This is Paul," he said, stepping back into the hallway.

"Paul, this is Randall Walls. I'd like to meet with you as soon as possible."

"Randall, this really isn't a good time," Paul said. "I'm at the hospital and they are getting ready to release the kids. My mother-in-law just arrived; can it wait a couple of days?"

Walls was silent for a moment. "Paul, this is important. Could you do it this evening? I wouldn't press but... this is important."

Paul took a deep, exasperated breath, glanced at his watch and said, "It better be. Okay, let me get the family settled and I'll call you back. We can probably meet around six if that is good for you."

"I'll wait on your call," Walls said and broke the connection.

*****

Walls was bent over in conversation with a man Paul didn't recognize. They stood and Walls said, "I want you to meet a friend of mine, Dr. Jerome Morrell. He's a professor of archaeology and an adjunct English instructor at the Institute. He also has some expertise that is a little unusual... crypto-archaeology. He has explored many of the more 'unconventional' theories, conspiracies and interesting ideas. Coffee's ready if you're interested."

They poured hot, dark coffee into standard issue academic ceramic mugs. Paul sized up Morrell; solidly built, sporting a mustache and although he had a ready smile, his eyes glinted darkly. "Call me Jerry."

Paul felt a firm handshake and somehow... a familiarity. Morrell, somehow, reminded Paul of John Rourke. It wasn't anything physical... they were different as day and night, but there was something about him.

As they all took seats at the conference table, Morrell spoke, "Archaeology is giving us a window into the 'real' past of our world and our species. OOPArts have made us question our view of the old world, for a long time."

"You used the term OOPArt; what is that?" Paul said, still a bit confused, taking another sip of the dark brew. "And how does it relate to the issue at hand?"

"It means an out-of-place artifact. The term was coined by American naturalist and cryptozoologist, Ivan T. Sanderson, for an object of historical, archaeological, or paleontological interest found in a very unusual or seemingly impossible context that could challenge conventional historical chronology by being 'too advanced' for the level of civilization that existed at the time; or showing 'human presence' well before humans were supposed to exist."

"Got an example?"

Morrell smiled. "The titanium sheets Dr. Rourke found are OOPArts. Another is the Antikythera mechanism, a clockwork-like device that dates to about a thousand years before clocks were invented. Many consider it to be evidence of alien visitation, while some argue it is a product 'not of man, but of the gods.' Mainstream scientists consider the Antikythera mechanism to be a form of mechanical computer, based on the theories of astronomy and mathematics, and developed by the ancient Greeks. Its design and workmanship reflect a previously unknown, but not implausible, degree of sophistication."

Morrell continued, "Look, modern man's history has been debated for years. When did he appear, how did he spread, and the most interesting is, how many families of man were there? Archaeology has found some answers but, quite frankly, those answers did not always jive with what we thought we know."

"For example, in China's Tarim Basin, blue-eyed mummies with red and blonde hair, who lived between 2,000 to 4,000 years before the Night of the War, over 100 of them have been found. They had long noses, deep set eyes and other unmistakably Aryan features. That discovery really shook up conventional thinking concerning the spread of mankind, trade and a host of other issues."

Walls took over the conversation, "In 1912, near Lake Delavan, Wisconsin, bodies from a 'lost race of giants' were found in burial mounds... supposedly. The enormous size of the skeletons and elongated skulls found did not fit very neatly into the textbook standard. They were enormous; between seven and a half to ten feet and their skulls, 'presumably those of men are much larger than the heads of any race which inhabit America today.'"

Morrell nodded. "Have you ever heard of Tollund Man?"

"Yes, a mummified body discovered about 1950, by two men cutting peat near the village of Tollund, Denmark." Growing impatient, Paul said, "Fascinating I'm sure, but again, how does this apply to the issue at hand?"

"Give me a few more minutes to explain," Morrell said. "We haven't scratched the surface yet." Morrell smiled. "Simply put, Mr. Rubenstein... much of what we think we know about our own history, is wrong. Shared legends, aliens, the Nazca Lines; there are a thousand different mysteries we have never unraveled. And now we know, without a doubt, that there is an alien presence on the planet."

Morrell sat his elbows on the table and formed a steeple with his outstretched fingers. "Let's say that the world governments knew and kept secret alien contact. Let's say the aliens offered to help us if the world governments agreed to dismantle their nuclear weapons. Then, let's say the governments reneged on the deal..."

"And the Night of the War was their reward?" Paul asked. Morrell shrugged and nodded at the same time.

Chapter Thirty-Five

John Rourke stared at the closed door for several minutes before attempting to get up. He eased his legs over the side of the examination table and slid off, holding onto the table for support. His head felt foggy, and fearing vertigo, he moved slowly and deliberately. *Well,* he thought, *that was very interesting. Wonder what in the hell is going on.* After a minute or so, the nausea disappeared and he took a couple of tentative steps. Convinced he was stable enough to explore, Rourke examined the room.

Sterile metal met his gaze at all levels. *Not stainless steel,* he thought, *this stuff is actually warm to the touch.* Except for the examination table the room was devoid of furnishings of any kind. Suddenly, there was a whishing sound behind him; turning, he saw the alien creature step in as the door closed. Rourke slowly edged back against the far wall with his fists clenched and ready; the creature did not advance until John's back touched the wall.

The creature moved slowly to the examination table and laid a silver-colored headband on the table and stepped to the opposite side of the room. Pointing at the headband and then at John, the creature stood quietly, waiting for a long moment before repeating the gesture.

John opened his hands and moved to the table and touched the headband, looked quizzically at the creature whose large out-of-proportion head gave what could have been seen as a slight nod. Rourke picked up the headband, raised it over his head and looked at the creature again. The single nod was repeated; John looked at the device uncertainly. It was about an inch from top to bottom and open at the back, and about a sixteenth of an inch thick.

Well, he thought. *Obviously I'm supposed to put this on voluntarily. This creature seems content for me to make the decision on my own without any coercion. What's the worst thing that could happen? Well, let's see... how about total control of my brain? But I'm already a captive. I'm butt naked and obviously no threat to it, except physically. It could have just as easily placed this device on my head while I was out, but didn't.* Rourke made a quick decision and slid the headband into place on his own head. The effect was immediate.

The pain, he mentally screamed and collapsed.

*****

Far above the surface of Earth, The Keeper stumbled; and for an instant, an intense pain flashed through him. Within seconds it passed, and with the exception of a sheen of sweat that covered his face and slight vertigo, he showed no other outward symptom from the attack. One word formed unbidden in his mind, *John.*

Chapter Thirty-Six

After what had started out as a kidnapping, Beaux "Diddly" Delys and Tuviah Friedman had settled down and, instead of a confrontation, were actually having a conversation. "As I said, Mr. Delys, I work for an organization that hunts Nazis; more accurately, Neo-Nazis. Also as I said, I am not your enemy but I fear the enemy is at the gate. I am one of the Aqrab." Friedman smiled. "We are not what you would call a... well known entity; we seek neither acknowledgement nor accolades. We are deadly serious in our mission. We concern ourselves with beginnings and endings; we are unafraid of either and embrace both conditions."

"We focus on protection, not necessarily of the individual but the essence of the Jewish people. Your client could possibly be a threat to that mission. Herr Croenberg appears to have recently faked his death. For what purpose, at this moment, we don't know. We do know that he has resurfaced and immediately reached out to Mr. Rubenstein. My job is to determine if his attempt to contact Rubenstein might constitute a threat to Rubenstein, or the Rourkes. If so, my job is to eliminate that threat."

"I was made aware of Croenberg's true identity only after he sent me on this job," Beaux said. "I think you're barking up the wrong tree, Mr. Friedman. Croenberg did reach out to Rubenstein; I made Rubenstein aware of Croenberg's wish to speak with him through an old friend of mine. That friend works directly for President Rourke and the Secret Service. There's no way they would have allowed a meeting without making sure Mr. Rubenstein would be safe."

Friedman was silent; he sat, looking deep into Delys eyes for a long moment. Slowly he raised the lighter again, relit the bowl of his pipe and puffed the Meerschaum several times before saying, "Then it is possible my people have misinterpreted the threat. Interesting…"

"Have you contacted our government with your fears?" Delys asked.

"No," Friedman said. "That is not the way the Aqrab does things. We tend to have a more… unobtrusive method to our activities. However, if it is true we have misinterpreted this situation, that may become necessary."

Beaux nodded. "I am willing to help, if I can. How much can you tell me about what you think you have discovered?"

"Mr. Delys, I mean no offense. I am aware of your background and frankly I don't know how far to trust you. My other problem is if we are wrong about who is threatened, we're not wrong about a threat existing. It is conceivable we identified the wrong target."

Beaux held up his hands. "Don't trust me, I don't care. Let me put you into contact with my friend, have a conversation and the two of you work it out."

After several puffs on the Meerschaum, he nodded. "I believe that will be acceptable. How soon could I speak to your friend?"

Delys pulled his cell phone, dialed a number and handed it to Friedman. "How about right now?"

*****

Tim Shaw saw Delys' name on his caller ID and answered, "Yes, Beaux. What do you need?"

"Mr. Shaw, I'm afraid it is not Mr. Delys. My name is Tuviah Friedman and I believe I have information you would find interesting. It concerns Mr. Croenberg and Mr. Rubenstein; do I have your attention?"

92

Shaw said, "You do, Mr. Friedman." He scribbled a note and slid it across the desk to another agent. "Get a location on the caller, NOW!!!" was all it said. "Is Mr. Delys alright? Can I speak to him... please?"

Friedman handed the phone to Delys. "Tim, Beaux here."

"You okay?"

"Well things were looking like there could have been a problem, but they're okay right now. Tim, I think you need to meet with this guy and the sooner the better."

"Any idea what this is about?"

"Not much of one but this guy is not independent. He works for something called the Aqrab. Ever heard of them?"

Shaw signaled "hurry up" to the agent. "Yes, yes I have." The agent handed Shaw a note with an address. Shaw said, "Where does he want to meet?"

"Up to you."

"Any idea where you're located?"

"Let me let you talk with him," Delys said and handed the phone back.

"Yes Mr. Shaw, this is Tuviah."

"If we're going to be on a first name basis, you can call me Tim. If you will give me an address, I'll come to you; provided you give me your assurance that Beaux Delys is not in danger."

"I am certain that by now you have my location. Mr. Delys is in no danger and is free to leave with you. Shall I expect you in..." pulling an ancient gold pocket watch from his vest and opening it, Friedman said, "Shall I expect you in thirty minutes?"

Chapter Thirty-Seven

Plan A, to attack the government building during a speech by President Wolfgang Mann, was not going to work. Mann's Press Secretary just announced: "The President has cancelled the speech in view of a 'global emergency' and instead is meeting with his cabinet on matters of national security."

Burkholter, listening on the car radio, cursed. Pulling the citizen's band radio's microphone from the holder on the dash board, he keyed it and said, "Implement Plan B," and hung it back up.

Six civilian cargo vans of different color and signage moved from the government building six blocks away and converged on Bellevue, the Executive Mansion. Within minutes they were staged on side streets, equal distance from the residence and within three minutes driving time from it.

The rocket pod launchers in each van had been checked, double checked and triple checked. The drivers flipped switches on their dashes to the armed position, and picked up remote controls that would open the side doors automatically, allowing the unleashing of a hell-fire of nine 2.75 inch rockets at the target. First, the high explosive rounds would blast through the exterior of the brick and decorative stone building, opening a pathway for anti-personnel rounds and lastly, the incendiary rounds.

As the concussion and hail of shrapnel combined with the steel ball bearings and fléchettes, human flesh would be cooked in the flaming inferno. While the rockets were flying, the machine gunners would unleash a spray of .762 slugs at the residence and at any resistance that might be mounted by security.

The sheer devastation of the attack, designed to collapse the entire building and roast its occupants, would create terror. During that confusion and terror of the attack, the cargo vans would simply follow the traffic flow out of the area. Total elapsed time for the attack... less than three minutes and the President of New Germany would be dead, along with his wife Sarah.

Horst Burkholter would have his "total overkill and absolute revenge."

Chapter Thirty-Eight

A news alert announced the scheduling of a press conference by President Mann on a nation security condition at 6:00 P.M. this evening. The pretty Press Secretary, a diminutive blond, was fielding questions from the press corps' representatives of New Germany's news agencies.

"Can you tell us what the security condition involves?" The question came from in back of the room.

"At this time, all I can tell you is that there are concerns about the disease outbreak in Hawaii. While we have not had any instances here, the President wants to be prudent and address potential concerns should the disease manifest here. These are purely reasonable concerns and more prophylactic than crisis in nature. The President is meeting with his cabinet this afternoon and following that meeting, will make the announcement."

"Word has reached us that the First Lady might be ill," said the anchor from NGTV. "Any relationship to this situation?"

The Press Secretary smiled. "None at all. I have spoken with the First Lady and she is resting well. As you know, there have been issues in Hawaii... Let me address that also, because there is a relationship there. Mrs. Mann's grandchildren, niece and nephew, were victims of a heinous kidnapping." The floor buzzed.

Holding her hand to quiet the reporters, the Secretary continued, "All of the children have been successfully rescued and the perpetrators apprehended. The children have been checked by Hawaiian medical teams and declared totally fine. Admittedly, this caused strain and worry for the First Lady. She is resting quietly and looking forward to seeing them in the very near future."

"Any word on John Rourke?" came the follow up question.

Surprised by the question, the Secretary shifted through her notes to gain composure before answering.

Smiling, she said, "Dr. Rourke, according to latest information, is on an archeological expedition to Mount Rushmore in what was South Dakota. It appears the expedition, which was launched by the American Government to retrieve national treasures that had been secured in the monument just before the Night of the War, has been successful. Unfortunately, we have not been contacted by Dr. Rourke, seems a weather condition in the area has caused some communications problems. We have been assured there are no reasons for concern."

"Is the President meeting with the Cabinet now?"

She checked her watch. "As a matter of fact, that meeting is scheduled to start in the next twenty minutes. That's all for today, thank you."

She turned and left the podium, headed directly to the President's office, and knocking once, she entered. "Sir, I wanted to let you know we just had a question about Dr. Rourke."

Wolfgang Mann frowned. "Hate to hear that, I guess I better get in touch with President Rourke. We may need to get ahead of this sooner than we thought. Thank you."

She nodded and closing the door wondered, *What do we tell the world if he is really gone?*

Chapter Thirty-Nine

When the local TV station announced the Presidential press conference, Burkholter smiled. Turning to Vale he said, "If the conference is scheduled for 6:00 this evening, we will attack Bellevue at 4:30. They will still be meeting and we know where they'll be."

Vale returned the smile, stood and said, "Good luck my friend. It is a beautiful day for revenge." He gave the Nazi salute and said, "Heil Hitler," and left the run-down, single-story home Burkholter used for his headquarters. Checking his watch, he headed to the airport, two hours to catch a flight and be out of New Germany before all hell broke loose.

Burkholter made three phone calls, giving a single word to each that would activate the mission. He smiled; he would be driving one of the vans himself. Aloud he said, "Today... today we will fire the first shots in the battle to reinstitute the Reich." He was too stupid to feel anxiety, only an adrenal rush.

*****

The meeting had started on time, and for two hours, Wolfgang Mann sat quietly taking in information; it seemed like days. Checking his watch, he realized he still had almost two hours left before the press conference. Clearing his thoughts, he said, "Ladies and Gentlemen, thank you for your inputs." Holding up his watch, he continued, "I believe that we should now focus on what I'm going to say to our citizens. I would like to wrap this up by 5:30 and get a moment of peace before I broadcast our findings."

"I'd like for our Chairman of Emergency Services, to lay out what steps we will be advising our citizens of; that will be the most important part of the broadcast." Willie Schultz, PhD, MD, stood and passed out two sheets of paper. He spoke for almost thirty minutes, uninterrupted. At the end of Schultz's presentation, President Mann rose from his seat and walked to the podium.

The first rocket slammed into the Presidential residence, tearing through the brick and stone veneer and exploded in the main lobby. Suddenly the electricity was off, smoke was filling the air. For a second there was total silence, then another explosion and the silence was slashed by shouts and screams competing for dominance in the pandemonium. More explosions could be heard, and felt, on all sides of the building. Sheet rock dropped from the ceiling, the chandeliers rocked and crashed to the floor. Shrapnel whistled through the air, tearing chunks from the walls, ripping through bodies and sending blood in ghoulish sprays.

The impacts were focused on the ground floor; support beams were blown apart; and from the outside, fires could be seen on all floors. Structural integrity was lost half way through the attack, as parts of the second and third floors sagged under their own weight; then fell, smashing into the first floor.

In less than five minutes, the building was in total ruin. Part of the North wall still stood, all three stories of it. The pile of debris belched tongues of fire and plumes of smoke in dozens of places. In ones and twos, people somehow crawled and clawed their way out of the debris. Torn, scraped and bleeding, they stumbled and crawled to safety... wherever that was. The stench of burning human flesh permeated the air and drifted across the streets. After the incredible sounds of explosions, gunfire and the building collapsing, the quiet was almost startling.

Then, in the distance, the first sirens could be heard headed that way.

People across the streets, around the residence, began picking themselves up off the ground and from behind cars where they had jumped for safety or been knocked by the concussions of rockets; at least the ones that could. Shrapnel had visited devastation not only inside the building, but outside. Many people still lay on the streets and in yards and passageways; most unmoving, with body parts missing. Their clothes were either on fire or missing. Blood ran down the streets of New Germany's capital.

Chapter Forty

As intense and immediate as the pain in his head was, it was gone just as quickly. John Rourke couldn't tell if he had passed out or not. The creature looked at him. *My God,* Rourke thought, *I've never experienced anything like that.*

Has... the... pain... left... you? a voice said in Rourke's head. He turned to look at the creature.

"Is that you I hear?" Rourke said in a whisper. The creature gave what could have been seen as a slight nod of its large head.

Has... the... pain... left... you?

"Yes, it has," Rourke said, weakly. "Will it come back?"

Not... as... long... as... the... device... is... in... place.

Rourke nodded. "That is good to know, I'll leave it alone for right now. You are not speaking, are you?"

Not... as... your... people... do. This... will... suffice... will... it... not?

"Yes, it will suffice. How do you know my language?"

It... is... the... device. It... allows... us... to... communicate.

"Why am I here? What is it that you want from me?"

Understanding...

"Understanding of what?"

Understanding... of... what... is... real.

Stronger now, Rourke sat up. He stood slowly until he faced the creature, full on. "I understand that you are at war with my people. I understand you are war with my very world."

This... is... not... accurate.

"I know this war started over forty thousand of our years ago. And your kind started it."

This... is... not... accurate.

Rourke stared at the creature, he thought, *Can you read my thoughts?* There was no response. *Can you read my thoughts?* No response, he said aloud, "Can you read my thoughts?"

No... that... would... not... be... appropriate.

"But, I can hear you in my mind?"

Our... bodies... are... different... Your... people... communicate... verbally... mine... do... not. The... device... allows... you... to... hear... my... thoughts... it... does... not... allow... me... to... hear... yours.

Rourke tried to analyze the sound in his mind; it was somewhat mechanical, but not in the usual sense. It also had the characteristics of the chirping made by crickets in the evening. Not unpleasant, simply not human.

"Why am I here? What is it that you want from me?"

Understanding... there... is... no... purpose... in... conflict.

"You started this conflict, not us," Rourke said, a hint of steel in his voice.

This... is... not... accurate.

"You started this by using those of our people you cloned from the Eden Mission. You used them to attack us," Rourke said. "I was there; I have captured some of them. You used some kind of mind control on them."

This... is... not... totally... accurate.

Rourke glared but the creature did not move. "Okay, tell me then, which parts are not accurate."

My... attempts... to... establish... contact... between... our... races... was... misinterpreted... by... your... people... because... of... the... others.

"It failed because your clones were faulty? Is that what you want me to believe?"

Partially... but... that... is... not... accurate. I... speak... also... of... the... others... the... old... ones... who... came...before.

Rourke didn't understand. "What others, which old ones?" The creature didn't speak, instead it raised one arm and with one elongated finger pointed up. Rourke frowned. "I don't understand?"

The... others... the... old... ones. Those... who... have... returned.

The creature, Rourke figured out, had not been pointing at the ceiling; it meant the sky. "Are the others, the old ones, the creatures we know as the KI?"

The creature gave a slight nod of its large head.

Rourke looked thoughtfully at the creature. "Our species are very different."

Not... so... different. The creature laid its hand on the wall of the chamber. Something Rourke recognized as a hologram appeared. Do... you... know... this?

"It is the double helix we call DNA. It is the genetic map of our bodies."

Accurate... this... is... the... one... for... your... species. A second hologram appeared. This... is... the... one... for... mine.

Rourke stared then walked to study the two rotating images. His mind began dredging up what he remembered about the structure, the gnome of life. After several minutes, he turned to the creature. "They appear very close and the general structure is identical. I assume the differences are at the chromosome level or sub-chromosome level," he said, looking back at the hologram and studying it closer.

We... are... not... so... different... from... you. The... differences... are... small... in... comparison... to... our... similarities.

"But," Rourke's mind was spinning now. "How is that possible?"

It... is... simple. We... were... created... as... your... species... was. The... same... way. We... and... all... sentient... life... forms. More... similar... than... different.

Rourke thought a moment. "Our species is thought by some to have evolved. Others believe we were created by God. Are you familiar with that concept?"

God... that... is... accurate.

Rourke was stunned. "Are you saying God is real. Are you saying He also created your people?"

God... that... is... accurate. All... peoples... everywhere.

"Tell me," Rourke said. "Why the invasion of my planet, and why now?"

Invasion… that... is... not... accurate.

Rourke thought for a moment. *Semantics*? Possibly, maybe another word would be more accurate. "Why did you come to my world now?"

That... is... not... accurate. We... have... always... been... here. Your... world... my... world... all... worlds... part... of... the... same... The creature did not finish the phrase.

Rourke tried, "Your world, my world, all worlds, part of the same, plan?"

That... is... accurate. All... peoples... all... different... all... the... same. We... each... world... each... individual... creature... chose... be... good... or... not... good. Our... choice.

"Free will?" Rourke asked. "You are saying, your people—my people—we all have free will?"

The creature gave a slight nod of its large head.

Chapter Forty-One

"What... What the hell did you say?" Michael Rourke screamed at his Press Secretary.

Paul Dunlap stood bracing himself and said, "Early reports are not good, Sir. About ten minutes ago, the Bellevue was hit by a well-coordinated heavy attack using rockets and machine gunfire. The structure itself has mostly collapsed. First responders are on the scene and full medical is still arriving."

"Son of a..." Michael caught himself. "Is there any word on Wolf?"

Dunlap shook his head. "There has been no word on President Mann as of yet. The number of survivors from the building itself is as yet unknown. Operations are being divided between rescue and recovery. Sir, right now, that is all we have. Part of it came from our embassy, but most we got off the newscasts."

Michael took a deep breath. "Okay, Paul, I want you to personally stay on this and report directly to me. You say it is already on the TV?" Dunlap nodded. "Let the First Lady know, and tell her I want her here with me. Get in touch with Tim Shaw and tell him I want a blanket of security around my family. Tell the Joint Chiefs I want security at all of our bases upgraded immediately. Let Mid-Wake know and have them standing by. I want Combat Air Patrols over our Capital initiated immediately, and shut down all commercial air flights."

Michael took a deep breath and picked up his desk phone and began dialing. "Paul, right now you have to excuse me, I have to notify my mother..." Dunlap turned and closed the door, just as he heard the President say, "Mom, please sit down, I need to tell you something..."

Chapter Forty-Two

Traffic had been rerouted and police had set up a six block cordon around the building, or what was left of it. When the first Emergency Responders screeched to a halt outside the Executive Mansion, at first, they just stood, staring. The devastation was more complete than any of them had imagined or expected. After a moment of disbelief and shock, training took over; they ran toward what little was left of the building.

The first Fire Captain on the scene called for all fire battalions to respond, except two on the outskirts of town. They would be responsible for handling any emergency of a normal nature that developed. He had Dispatch contact several construction companies and ordered them to respond with bulldozers, cranes and all the heavy equipment they had. Then he climbed down from his truck and stood there, looking.

Adjacent buildings and cars were on fire, pedestrians lay everywhere, either dead or wounded. Those who were ambulatory stumbled around in a state of shock, blank stares on their faces. *Where the hell do we even start?* he thought. Sadly, he decided it really didn't make any difference, he just had to start. So he walked to the ruins with a bullhorn and started directing operations.

Mass casualty incidents can best be described as chaos, trying to be interrupted by action. Paramedics, first aid squads, emergency squads, rescue squads, ambulance service, not to mention police and fire had to establish a beginning place. The first goal was to gain control and keep more injuries and deaths from occurring.

Medical services focused on providing treatment for those in need of urgent medical care and transporting the injured to hospitals and emergency rooms. The sheer number of victims was overwhelming.

Crews were triaging the victims, taking no more than one minute per patient. Three things were checked: breathing, circulation, and consciousness and assigning one of four color-coded triage levels. The lowest level is called "Dead/Non-Salvageable" and were "Black Tagged." These were obviously deceased, or had injuries so severe that care would require more effort than is practical.

Patients needing cardiopulmonary resuscitation would be "Black Tagged" because at least one responder would have to treat them and not be able to assist other people.

"Walking Wounded" or "Green Tagged," had minor injuries and could get out of the incident area and to a treatment area under their own power. "Delayed Treatment" or "Yellow Tagged," had non-life-threatening injuries, but couldn't get to a treatment area under their own power.

"Immediate Treatment" or "Red Tagged" was the highest level of triage; it was for major life-threatening injuries but they are "salvageable." These people need immediate advanced care, but could wait until additional crews arrive. Triage came down to decisions on who does and does not receive treatment, and started by the first two or three crews that arrived on-scene.

Not sure if there were chemical or biological hazards, the Fire Captain ordered a clean zone set up roughly two to three hundred yards from the incident, and uphill and upwind from the incident. This also held the incident command post. The entire immediate area around Bellevue was declared a "hot zone" until it was determined if it needed decontamination.

Within the first two hours, 237 were triaged. Forty-seven bodies were found on the streets and areas immediately adjacent to the residence. Trailers of heavy equipment arrived, and search teams tried to find victims in the rubble but fires hampered their efforts. It appeared that twelve of the people from inside Bellevue had escaped. They had literally clawed their way out of the building or had been blown physically out of the building by explosions before the top two floors collapsed.

Neither the President, nor his cabinet or any member of the Executive Mansion staff, had been found, yet.

Chapter Forty-Three

Sarah Rourke-Mann, First Lady of New Germany, gripped the overhead handles in Paul Rubenstein's speeding vehicle; her knuckles as white as her drained complexion. "Paul, be careful," she said. Rubenstein grunted and pressed his foot tighter to the floor, trying to keep up with the escort vehicle ahead of him. That vehicle was running with flashing lights and the siren at full blast, clearing a way to the Capital... and her son, Michael.

Michael Rourke sat in his office, surrounded by a cacophony of noise. In the corner was a television with the latest images of Bellevue, smoking and still. Tongues of several small fires still burned in the ruins. An army of humans and K-9s searched, climbing over the ruins like ants searching for sugar. A dozen cell phone conversations were going on simultaneously, each caller trying to make him or herself heard above other voices, the television, the beeping of laptops and the ringing of the President's desk phone.

It was pandemonium.

The Marine Guard in the hallway opened the door to the office, caught the President's eye and nodded once. Michael stood up and walked into the hall and straight into his mother's arms.

"What do we know, Michael?" she asked.

"Come with me, Mother." Michael guided her and Rubenstein into an empty office two doors down and closed the door. "Here's what we know right now," he said. "Bellevue was attacked by several vehicles that circled on the roundabout, firing rockets and machine guns. From everything I have seen and been told, the attack was... devastating. The top two floors collapsed, crushing the main floor."

"Wolfgang..." tears jumped back into her eyes. "What about Wolf?"

Michael shook his head. "Nothing right now, first responders are trying to go through the rubble in a search for survivors. As of now, they haven't found Wolf or anyone else." Michael looked at Sarah and asked, "What's that Dad always said, 'While I breathe, I hope?'"

Sarah nodded stiffly.

"Then right now all we can do... all you can do is hope... and pray."

Paul interjected, "Do we know who's responsible?"

"Neo-Nazis, it appears," Michael said, turning to Paul. "Photographic analysis indicates they probably were connected to the group that grabbed Mom at the school. We have identified Horst Burkholter, the older brother of Johann Burkholter and Helmut Freed. Freed's brother, Franz, was the one who Dad shot through the elbow when he rescued Mom. Johann was the one Dad referred to as Woody the Wood Pecker. They were driving the first two vehicles; the other four drivers have not been identified, yet."

Sarah moved and stood directly in front of Michael. "What are his chances, Michael? And tell me the truth."

Michael put his hands on her shoulders, took a deep breath and said as softly as he could, "Mom, honestly it doesn't look good. However, survivors are often found in collapsed buildings hours or even days afterward. Some injured, some saved from being crushed by furniture, a stairwell... One woman survived last year after the attack on the Capitol because she was at a soft drink vending machine when part of the roof came down. The machine was partially crushed but there was a small area in which she survived. It was several hours, however, before the rescuers found her. Maybe we'll be lucky."

She smiled, fondly. "Lucky, you know what Wolf told me right before I left? He said at his age, getting lucky was remembering why he had walked into a particular room." Through her smile, tears started down her cheeks and she hugged him tightly. Over her shoulder, Michael looked directly into Paul's eyes. Paul shook his head slowly and Michael gave a small nod. Paul wrapped his arms around both of them.

Chapter Forty-Four

That evening, Michael walked to the podium in the briefing room. The quickly scheduled Press Conference was one he wished he didn't have to make. In a suit as dark as his mood, he stood in front of the Presidential Seal. He looked at his notes for several seconds then directly at the television camera.

"My fellow Americans, today is a difficult one for the people of New Germany and my family. First of all let me say, our condolences... our sincere condolences go out to the families suffering through the loss of a loved one. We offer a prayer to those families waiting on word on friends and family members currently listed among the missing."

"The First Lady of Germany, Sarah Rourke-Mann, my mother, is safe. In fact, she was staying with my wife and me following the rescue of my half-brother and sister, and my niece and nephew early this week. She asked that I speak directly to the citizens of her adopted country."

Picking up a note card, Michael said, "These are her words: 'Citizens of New Germany. My heart hurts along with you as I wait for word about my husband, Wolfgang, and our many friends and colleagues at the Presidential residence. As you know, I normally leave political issues to my husband. Unfortunately, our government must now struggle to reform and... where necessary, replace a majority of our legislators and leaders. Now, more than ever... we must remain strong. We must remain united and we must pray that somehow, under the debris, there are survivors. Stay strong my people, I will be returning to my adopted land as soon as possible. It is my place to stand with you. You are in my prayers.'"

Michael laid down the card and said, "The terror events of the past hours, in New Germany, have shown some problems. While it has been proven repeatedly that the authorities have been very good, most of the time, at stopping large and well organized groups of terrorists, our abilities to prevent a self-motivated, small terrorist group are severely hampered. We recognize that has to be improved for us to continue to enjoy a relatively free society. At the same time, I doubt any citizen is interested in trading freedom for complete safety... or actually, the illusion of safety.

"Laws and regulations, and even responsible humanity, have no effect on those who have decided to become terrorists. These people are dedicated not to the rule of law, not to the common good, but to their own particular and peculiar dogmas. No country could have prevented this small marginally skilled group of Neo-Nazi fanatics from attacking the governmental structure of New Germany.

"While as noble, unselfish and courageous as the responding units were, they were nothing more than a reactive force. They were not, and are not, a preventive force. Our first responders have always, and will always, arrive too late. They arrive after the fact.

"These points have not been challenged by anyone that has studied the reality of these events. The mere fact that many of the leaders of the free world refuse to actually name the enemy, labeling them as 'outlaws,' 'nationalists' or 'extremists,' does nothing more than promote the continued slaughter of innocent citizens and non-combatants. That means simply it will continue until we do submit to the terrorists' unrealistic and changing goals, or die. We will not do either."

Michael looked up and said, "I will now open it up for questions."

Bill Nolan, from DOT Television said, "Mr. President, one report I've read suggests assigning a counter-terrorist operator to each likely target in our own government. Is that being considered?"

Michael said, "First of all, while our security condition has been raised, we have no indication of a potential attack here. Bill, a plan like that would be as ineffective as it is impossible. No nation has those kinds of resources, the sheer numbers it would require. It is not practical and no, it is not being considered."

"Follow up then, Mr. President," Nolan said. "What is being considered?"

Michael pondered the question before answering. "Coordinated preventative steps combined with personal responsibility. That is the only true alternative. But it is an alternative that frightens many world leaders whose vocabulary does not include the words 'Lone Wolf Terrorist.'"

Michael looked directly at the camera. "Therefore, the phrase 'Lone Wolf Counter-Terrorist' must be placed in our vocabularies."

Agnes Briggs, from Honolulu's largest newspaper shouted, "What does that term mean?"

Michael turned to her and smiled. "Agnes, this will not be popular with my critics but let me explain. At any terror event, unfortunately there have always been plenty of everyday 'people.' Unfortunately, the majority end up as faceless victims, remembered only by their families and otherwise lost to the dusty annals of historical accounts."

"But, there have always been a few whose initial reaction was not to cower and to shrink from the face of evil. They act and act bravely. It is possible their initial reactions are based on nothing more than simple anger; I don't know. But I do know that when they are unarmed because of legal restrictions or social norms or political correctness... they are without any effective means to act, and they are forced into victimhood."

"Today we live in dangerous times, as exemplified by what happened in New Germany. These dangerous times call for dangerous measures. If fact, they scream for them and the scream of humanity must be louder than the screams of those we lost today."

"That sound like vigilantism," someone hollered from the back of the room.

"Maybe... maybe it does," Michael sighed, "but right now I believe we must change our own tactics. It is time for every man or woman outraged by these events to take steps on their own... to become their own rescuer... their own counter-terrorist. The skills and abilities of these self-motivated killers are not nearly as high as the uninformed commentators of our news agencies would have us believe. Have the terrorists been effective? Partially.

"Do they know how to attack and destroy? Absolutely, but they are neither invulnerable nor all powerful. Witness how many photographs were taken, not only today, but each time there has been a terrorist or active shooter situation. The photos taken during this brutal attack are being analyzed as we speak and will, I am confident, identify these animals and lead to their arrests and ultimate punishment."

Nolan raised his hand again. "Do we know why the attack occurred? Did they have demands that were known?"

Michael nodded. "We have read their published manifesto and I assure you, this incident will not be the last. Therefore, I recommend that every capable man and woman within the sound of my voice arm themselves no matter what country they are in, obtain a weapon and the training necessary to be responsible and safe with that weapon and carry that weapon with them every single place they go. Anywhere a Lone Wolf, Home-Grown Terrorist may strike; a Home-Grown Counter-Terrorist must be ready."

"Mr. President, it sounds like you want to see a return to the old west," Agnes said, her glasses down low on her nose, her eyes wide above them in her haughty "signature look."

Michael addressed her head on. "Agnes, what I am saying is enough is enough. I find it foolish to waste time to define or understand why a shark attacks. It attacks because it is a shark. We need to develop the mindset and attitude to kill the terrorists, wherever and whenever they appear. That is the day this tide will begin to change. Too long we have lived in fear of the terrorists —the terrorists must learn to fear US. As we fear not knowing when or where the terrorists will strike; let the terrorists fear our abilities to strike back, harder and swifter than we ever have."

"Thank you everyone, please hold your children extra close tonight and send a prayer for our allies, our brothers and sisters in New Germany. Thank you."

Michael turned and walked out of the room. It was getting late and he still had a lot to do.

Chapter Forty-Five

Tuviah Friedman opened the door. "Mr. Shaw, it is a pleasure to meet you, even if the circumstances could be better."

Shaw noticed they were back to using surnames and that tickled him, he wasn't in a mood for cordiality. "Mr. Friedman, let's get down to business. We Americans don't take kindly to folks that come in and attempt to kidnap our citizens at gunpoint. What the hell is going on?"

"A Neo-Nazi threat we believed to be directed at Paul Rubenstein and led by Otto Croenberg. I believe now our theory was incorrect in that Mr. Rubenstein was not to be the target and Croenberg was not the perpetrator. The problem is we have intelligence that shows an increase of 'chatter' and activity on the parts of operatives belonging to a man named Peter Vale."

"I can tell you that Croenberg is definitely not involved," Shaw said. "In fact, it seems you and he are working on the same problem; the same threat... just two different tracks. So if Paul is not the target, who the hell is?"

Friedman hung his head, looked up and said, sadly, "I don't know. I think it may be practical to speak with Croenberg. It is possible each of us has only partial information that when put together will present a whole picture. You are aware of this person called Peter Vale? Vale is an avowed Neo-Nazi... We believe the threat is real and coming soon."

"I know of him."

"We suspected there was a connection between him and Otto Croenberg," Friedman said.

Shaw shook his head. "As I said, I suspect the only connection is that they both are, and have been, associated with the Neo-Nazi movement. However, I can tell you that Croenberg has tried to eliminate their influence in the Democratic Republic of Germany. That is what caused him so many problems."

Friedman puffed his Meerschaum. "You are saying that was the rationale behind his leaving office?"

"Also the rationale behind his faked suicide," Shaw said. "As soon as he was able, he tried to establish contact with Rubenstein and warn the Rourkes about Vale. We know that Vale has been in and out of Hawaii several times in the recent past. We suspect he was involved with the attack in New Germany and has now returned to the DRG."

"If accurate, that would align with information," said Friedman. "It is... I suppose possible that the intent of Croenberg's contact with Rubenstein was misinterpreted. However, I have it on good authority that Vale is returning to Hawaii; he may already be here. Could it be that he is working behind the scenes for a similar attack on the American government?"

Shaw frowned. "If he is... he is going to be met with a lot more resistance than he had in New Germany. President Mann had no intelligence that a new threat was possible. We do." Shaw stood. "If you will excuse me, I believe I should contact my people. I don't want a repeat of the attack at Bellevue."

Chapter Forty-Six

General Sullivan sat across from President Rourke. Sullivan wanted and had proposed a strong force be sent to New Germany to establish control; the President had disagreed. "Their recovery is their challenge to accomplish," Michael said. "The government is in chaos and there has been no request received, as yet. I will, however, discuss your suggestion with my mother."

Sullivan pushed, just a little. "But Sir, if there is no government, it could be perceived as a big help and assistance."

Michael smiled. "Remember General, right now the First Lady of New Germany is right here. She is the only recognized member of that government, and she assured me the anti-government faction that has so long opposed any move my step-father favored, would call such a force an invasion force. No, we will offer aid and assistance but not a large or recognizable military presence."

"Would you authorize advisors?" Sullivan asked.

"Yes."

"What about logistical support for medical services and supplies?"

Michael nodded. "Absolutely, I have already advised the Secretary of the Navy to send a carrier group to South America."

Sullivan nodded. "Would it be permissible to include the 442nd?"

Michael thought for a moment. "You mean the Dog Soldiers?"

Sullivan nodded.

Michael stood up and went to the window and stared out into the night. "Hmmm," Michael said, before turning back to the General. "Frank, I see what you're trying to do." Sullivan started to object but Michael silenced him with a hand wave. "Actually, I think this has some pretty good points.

Michael smiled. "You know my dad told me a story about a friend he had when he was young, someone that thought outside the box. The kid was about eighteen and living back home and he bought a horse from a farmer for a hundred dollars. The farmer agreed to deliver the horse the next day. But the next day the farmer drove up and said, 'Sorry son, but I have some bad news... the horse died.'"

"The guy replied, 'Well, then just give me my money back.'"

"The farmer said, 'Can't do that. I went and spent it already.'"

"The guy said, 'Ok, then, just bring me the dead horse.'"

"The farmer asked, 'What ya gonna do with him?'"

"The guy said, 'I'm going to raffle him off.'"

"The farmer said, 'You can't raffle off a dead horse!'"

"The guy said, 'Yes, I can. Watch me. I just won't tell anybody he's dead.'"

"A month went by and when the farmer met up with the young man again, he asked, 'What happened with that dead horse?'"

"The guy smiled and told the farmer, 'I raffled him off. I sold five hundred tickets at two dollars apiece and made a profit of $898.'"

"The farmer said, 'Didn't anyone complain?'"

"'Sure, but just the guy who won. So I gave him his two dollars back.' You're thinking outside that box, the Dog Soldiers aren't a substantial force but they are awfully good. Might not be a bad idea to have such a strike force nearby, should it be needed."

"That's what I'm thinking, Sir. Between SEALS and Special Operators already assigned to the carrier..."

Michael smirked, "I can hear my critics now, 'Have you heard the latest dumb stunt Rourke has pulled? He has sent an aircraft carrier to South America to help the bombing victims. What does he intend to do, bomb them?'"

Sullivan said, "Sir, I have your answer to that kind of criticism. Each of our carriers has a minimum of three hospitals on board that can treat several hundred people. Being nuclear powered they can supply free emergency electrical power to shore facilities. They have an average of at least three cafeterias with the capacity to feed 3,000 people, three meals a day.

"They can produce several thousand gallons of fresh water from sea water each day. They carry half a dozen helicopters for use in transporting victims and injured to and from their flight deck. We have eleven such ships; how many does the rest of the world have?"

"Do it then, General, I like the way you think," Michael said and shook Sullivan's hand. "Just remember, General, most of this conversation will remain confidential."

"Roger that, Mr. President," Sullivan said with a smile as he was leaving. "Roger that."

Chapter Forty-Seven

A Marine orderly knocked on Michael's office door. "Come in."

The Lance Corporal marched to the President's desk and saluted. "Sir, you need to see this."

Michael returned the salute and took the report; a generalized break down in New Germany had begun. The report identified that protesters had seized several buildings, including the Ministry of Finance. They were demanding the release of dozens of protesters already in custody after clashes with police, and to stop further detentions.

Protestors were in control of several bank offices and when police reinforcements arrived, they set about dispersing the protesters and arresting another dozen or so. So far, about one hundred people had died; some fatally shot in the clashes, some by other means. The protests continued, fueling fears of further escalation. The ring leaders were blaming the deaths of "innocent civilians" on authorities, but authorities disputed that, saying the wounds were not caused by police weapons.

The protests had increased in violence again last night as the struggling government passed a curfew and began the process for new elections. It was a mob mentality phenomenon. Someone, believed to be the Neo-Nazi faction responsible for the initial attack, was manipulating the process. Mobs were much more easily manipulated than individuals.

Michael stood and walked to his window that faced out onto the South Lawn. *Okay,* he thought. *It begins, now what I have to do is figure out how to contain it... if it can be contained. If not, I have to figure out how to stop it... if it can be stopped. If neither is an option, I have to figure out how to kill or capture those responsible for this mayhem.*

He took a deep breath and released it slowly. *And whatever I do has to be done without dragging my country, or the world, back to the brink of a world war. No pressure there...*

Chapter Forty-Eight

Shaw had called Beaux Delys with an invitation for supper and drinks. "I need a break and I need a buddy, got some time?"

"Absolutely, where do you want to meet?" They settled on a place Shaw was familiar with, Papa Joseph's Pizzeria. Delys had almost not recognized Shaw as he walked through the door. He looked like hell.

The waiter took their order and brought a pitcher of beer for them to nurse while the pizzas cooked. "What's the matter, Tim? You don't look well." Shaw sat there; he looked tired, and thoughtful, almost pensive.

Shaw looked up. "Beaux, I'm tired. That's all. The stuff with the kids really hit me, now we have the mess in New Germany. I'm tired and I'm starting to forget things. There's so much... we have so many things hitting us. I feel sometimes like I'm having amnesia and déjà vu at the same time. When my memory slips, it feels like... sometimes I think I've forgotten 'this' before. Maybe I'm too old for this stuff." Wistfully, Shaw continued, "I'm tired and I'm frustrated; you know I'm not the most patient person in the world."

Delys nodded and said, "I can concur with that Tim."

"Shucks," Shaw said. "When I was little, my grandfather used to make me stand in a closet for five minutes without moving. He called it elevator practice and said it would teach me patience. It didn't work."

Delys leaned over and placed his hand on Shaw's shoulder. "The President and the country need you Tim, right now more than ever." Delys saw he needed to break Shaw's mood. He said, "Tim, is it true that, here in Hawaii, it only takes one word to say 'I Love You?'"

Shaw looked at Delys and smiled. "Yeah, but you can also say it with a pineapple and a twenty." Delys smiled, it had worked. Wistfully,

Shaw smiled back and said, "This getting old crap is coming at a really bad time! I thought about retiring and living off of my savings. Wasn't sure what I was gonna do that second week."

Delys laughed and said, "Maybe you need a hobby?"

Shaw lightened up, just a little. "I remember when I turned two, I got really anxious. I figured out I'd doubled my age in a year. I thought, 'If this keeps up, by the time I'm six I'll be ninety.' Now, I intend to live forever—so far, so good."

"I say again, maybe you need a hobby?" Delys asked.

Shaw smiled for the first time, "I have a hobby. I have the world's largest collection of sea shells. I keep it scattered on beaches all over the world. Maybe you've seen it."

"What about fishing?" Delys continued.

"Naw, there's a fine line between fishing and just standing on the shore looking like an idiot, and I'm not sure what it is." Shaw took another sip of beer.

Delys recognized what was happening, Shaw was peppering him with Wrightisms, and he decided to play along. "What about a woman?"

"Women, you can't live with 'em, can't shoot 'em. I once had a girlfriend but she was weird. One day she asked me, 'If you could know how and when you were going to die, would you want to know?' I said, 'No.' She said, 'Okay, forget it.' Another time, I almost had a psychic girlfriend, but she left me before we met."

"Beaux, you know how it is when you go to be the subject of a psychology experiment, and nobody else shows up, and you think maybe that's part of the experiment? I'm like that all the time."

"But you have a lot of experience in a lot of areas," Delys said with a smile, playing along and feeding Tim Shaw openings.

Shaw nodded. "Yeah, but experience is something you don't get until just after you needed it. And here it is Monday again, you know, Monday is an awful way to spend one-seventh of your life."

About then, the waiter returned with the pizzas. Shaw, more relaxed now, attacked his with a vengeance. Between bites, he started machine gunning Delys with Wrightisms, one after the other. "When everything seems to be going well, I realize I obviously overlooked something. When everything is coming my way, I'm in the wrong lane.

"Hey, did you hear there was a power outage at a department store yesterday? Twenty people were trapped on the escalators. My buddy got busted for counterfeiting. He was making pennies. They caught him because he was putting the heads and tails on the wrong sides. Did you know that most people quit looking for work when they find a job?"

Shaw took another bite of pizza and slugged the beer down, waving for the waiter, he signaled for another round. "Another thing, Mr. Overachiever, remember this, eagles may soar, but weasels don't get sucked into jet engines. Have you ever worried what happens if you get scared half to death, twice? And don't forget if at first you don't succeed, destroy all evidence that you tried. It is a fact that for every action, there is an equal and opposite criticism. It's okay to fall behind; the sooner you fall behind, the more time you'll have to catch up."

Delys was laughing; twice, he almost choked on the pizza. "Tell me some more of your philosophy."

"Okay," Shaw said. "But you probably should take notes. First of all, if you must choose between two evils, pick the one you've never tried before. Second, plan to be spontaneous... tomorrow. Only borrow money from pessimists, they don't expect it back. Remember, forty-two point seven percent of all statistics are made up on the spot and a conscience is what hurts when all your other parts feel so good."

Shaw was laughing with Delys now. He slapped the table. "You know, yesterday I saw a chicken crossing the road. I asked it why. It told me it was none of my business. I had some eyeglasses once, but I was walking down the street when suddenly the prescription ran out. Sometimes I try to daydream, but my mind just keeps wandering."

Shaw grew serious. "Hey, I just thought of something, if you tell a joke in the forest, but nobody laughs, was it a joke? You ever wonder if God dropped acid, would he see people? Ever thought of the fact that, in school, every period ends with a bell? Every sentence ends with a period but every crime ends with a sentence. And what the hell, if a word in the dictionary was misspelled, how would we know?"

By the end of the meal, Shaw was back to his old self. Shaw paid the bill and they stepped outside. Shaw lit a cigarette and turned to his old friend. "Beaux, I can't tell ya how much I needed tonight. Thanks for being there." Delys reached out his hand to Shaw and said, "Any time ..."

Suddenly, a single gunshot smashed the sound of the late night traffic and Delys collapsed on the cold, wet sidewalk.

Chapter Forty-Nine

Michael was... not quite so anxious. He was more concerned... more concerned than he had been since the attack on Bellevue; the world seemed to be unraveling, again. He had tossed and turned since 4:00 A.M.; he swung out of the bed he shared with Natalia and went to the small kitchen downstairs and turned on the coffee maker. He sat alone at the table, waiting for it to brew.

When the brew sounded three pings, it startled him. He rubbed his face with both hands, stood up and pulled a coffee mug from the cabinet and poured a cup. Sitting back down, he stared at the Presidential seal on the cup. "President..." he said in a low, somber tone. "President of the entire damn country and I'm sitting here pondering what the hell to do with my own kids. My own family."

"They're our kids, Mr. President," Natalia's voice came from the doorway, surprising Michael. He walked toward her; he took her in his arms and hugged her for several minutes, not speaking. Finally he released his grip and stepped back to look at her. "You know, even with no makeup, a pair of flannel pajamas, and bed mussed hair, I have to admit, you're still a knock out." She wasn't going to be distracted. "And, it's our family." She walked to the cabinet and pulled another mug down. "Do we need to talk?"

Michael nodded. "Didn't mean to wake you up, honey. I needed some alone time to think. Yes, I think we do need to talk."

Natalia poured coffee into her cup, stirred in a teaspoon of sugar and sat down, taking a sip. "How do you drink that stuff black?" she asked. "I mean, I did it when we were in the field all of the time. Now I like to treat myself."

"When we were in the field..." Michael said, his voice sounding haunted. "Do you remember, I mean do you really remember when we were in the field?"

She took another sip. "That's a silly question, of course I do. We were in danger all of the time, but we got through it. We got through it together, as a family."

Michael laughed. "And what a family it was in those days, before you and I married."

She looked at him, one eyebrow cocked. "Do you and I have a problem?"

Michael shook his head. "There is a problem, but it is not between you and me. Remember when we first met?"

Natalia smiled. "You were the cutest kid, so like your father; just a smaller reproduction of him. You were the bravest little guy I ever knew."

Michael smiled. "That was before the big sleep. The world had ended, Dad had sealed us all in the Retreat, in the cryogenic chambers, in the hope we might be able to survive the end of the world."

"And we did," she said, reaching over to touch his arm. "We did survive, Michael."

"Remember what it was like when you woke up?" He asked. "I was grown. Dad had awakened Annie and me and trained us how to survive, then he went back to sleep and we stayed awake, and practiced those skills until it was time for all of us to awaken."

She gazed deep into the sweet black coffee, swirling it around, remembering. "It was certainly a surprise. We had gone to sleep with you a little boy and awoke to you and Annie as adults. It wasn't easy."

Michael shook his head. "Mom never got over it. 'I lost their childhood' she said. Dad made a decision..."

"Like he always did, he can make decisions," she said.

"But was it fair for him to make that decision, without discussing it with her?"

"The world had ended, Michael. We had fought so hard for so long. He had searched for Sarah and you and Annie so hard," she said, softly. "He was simply planning ahead as he always did. He knew you and Annie would have a much better chance to survive whatever we found in the new world, if you were adults."

"Not just adults, Natalia," he said with emphasis. "Trained adults. Grownups with some abilities... some training. He was right of course, and yes it did work. We survived." Natalia simply stared at him, letting him pull his thoughts together. Michael said, "It was lonely those years for me and Annie, while the rest of you slept. All we could do was watch over you and improve on our skills."

"It's a good thing you two were watching or Paul would have died when his chamber malfunctioned. If it had not been for Annie's intuition..." She grew quiet.

"Yes, he would have died; he and Annie would never have married and we wouldn't have John Michael and Natalie," he said. "Then Mom got hurt and we went into the second sleep. Even when we woke up that time, the world was still crazy..." he stared off in the distance, somewhere.

"Michael," she said, "I think the world is always going to be a crazy place. But we don't have to be crazy just to live in it." She thought for a moment. "No, if Paul had died, we wouldn't have John Michael or Natalia. But he didn't and we do."

"That's the problem I'm struggling with." Michael snapped his eyes at her.

"I don't... I don't understand."

"We were responsible; we did wait for the craziness to die down." He started pacing. "For sixteen years, the world rocked along quite well.

Now, now look at us... I'm the President of the whole frigging country. Bellevue has been destroyed and we still don't know if Wolf is alive or buried in the rubble." He spun toward her. "And where the hell is my father?"

She had no idea how to help him. "John will be alright, Michael," she said. "He always is, you know that."

"Sure, he always HAS been," Michael said, leaning at the sink and staring out into the darkness through the window above it. For a long time, he stood, neither of them saying anything. Finally, slowly, he turned around. "What if his luck has finally run out? What if he got caught up in something he could not plan ahead for? What if..." He fought both for and against the next words. "What if he is dead?

"What if the world is going to go through another period of insanity? I'm looking at the same prospect that Dad did before our first sleep," he said, finally sitting back down. "What is the best thing I can do to give our children, all of our children, the best chance for survival?"

Natalia sat there for a long time; several minutes. She could hear and feel the anguish in his voice. Taking a deep breath, she asked, "Have you come up with anything?"

Michael stood and walked back to the window, he couldn't look at her when he said it, "I think so but I don't know how the rest of the family, the other parents—including you—are going to feel about it."

The dawn rays were beginning to streak across the sky as she joined him at the window. "Well," she said as she wrapped her arms around his mid-section and squeezed. "Well, maybe we need to call a family meeting and see."

Chapter Fifty

Helmut Schmidt, Wolfgang Mann's head of security, was on the verge of physical exhaustion. He had divided his time between overseeing the recovery effort, and making sure those government officials that remained were under a protective cloak. From all indications, unless someone was found alive, the government of New Germany had been virtually destroyed. *The President and Vice President along with the entire cabinet...* he took a long breath and wiped his face. *The President and Vice President along with the entire cabinet are dead,* he thought.

The next highest living official, The Federal Chancellor, Herr Conrad Ludenberg was the only other member of the Federal Government, besides the President, to be elected. It is the Chancellor who lays down the guidelines of government policy. That gave the Federal Chancellor a whole array of instruments of leadership which easily stands up to a comparison with the power of the President in a presidential democracy. Prior to the attack, Ludenberg had been fifth in line, so far as power was concerned. Today, he was number one.

Schmidt brushed the dust from his coveralls and removed them. Underneath, a pair of slacks and an open-neck shirt served as his uniform of the day. He left the ruins of Bellevue for his morning ritual. The Recovery Supervisor had told him privately, "Personally, Herr Schmidt, I hold no hope of finding anyone alive. While it is possible some miracle did happen..." He just shook his head.

The Chancellor had called for a meeting with Schmidt to discuss "options." There weren't any... none that Schmidt could see anyway.

Chapter Fifty-One

Michael called Annie, Paul and Emma. Sarah agreed to watch all the kids; she didn't want to get far from the phone anyway; in case there was word about Wolf. Now the morning of the second day since the attack... Sarah was losing hope that Wolfgang would be found alive.

Paul and Annie dropped their kids off when they picked Emma up to drive to the White House. Paul still didn't know how that name had stuck. The original White House had been destroyed during the Night of the War. Years later, when the government had been re-established in Hawaii, someone must have thought it appropriate to call this Presidential residence by the same name.

They drove through the private entrance gate, parked and strolled up the walkway to the private residence of the President and First Lady. As many times as they had been there, it still was an impressing event. Michael and Natalia's two children, John Paul and Sarah Ann, had locked themselves in the media room for an afternoon of movies and popcorn.

In Michael's private office, Paul, Annie and Emma were on the couch while Natalia and Michael sat in chairs on the other side of the coffee table. "First of all, Emma, we still have no word on Dad; sorry but we're still trying. Second, we still have no word on Wolfgang either. Several bodies and one survivor have been pulled from the rubble."

Paul said, "Thanks Michael. We knew this wasn't a meeting about them. What's going on?"

Michael looked at Natalia; she inclined her head in a gesture for him to begin. A knock came at the door.

"Come on in, Della," Michael said. Della, the senior member of the White House residential service staff, walked to the coffee table and set down a tray with refreshments. "Coffee anyone; pastries?"

Michael said, "Thank you Della. You may leave now, is the rest of the staff downstairs?"

"Yes Sir, per you instructions. The residence is clear."

Michael nodded. "Thank you Della, I'll buzz you when we're through."

Della excused herself and closed the door on the way out.

Michael said, "I've called this meeting because I want to ask your approval on something. I spoke with Natalia about this idea earlier this morning. I need your input before it goes any further."

Paul shifted and looked at Annie. "What is it, Michael?"

Natalia frowned and said, "Michael, get on with it."

Michael nodded. "Okay, I have something to discuss with you. An idea I want you to consider, seriously. It involves our children..."

Chapter Fifty-Two

Sarah laid little Eddie in his crib, she had finally been able to rock him to sleep as she kept softly singing a refrain from an old Andy Williams song, "Emily, Emily, Emily. As the murmuring sound of May..."

Focusing on the child had allowed her the pleasure of not thinking of anything else. Not Wolfgang... not the destruction at Bellevue... not John Rourke... nothing but the baby. The older children were outside in the backyard, playing. She stood at the double window, watching them, envying the innocence of youth. The phone rang on the kitchen counter and she walked over to it. "Hello."

A deep but resonant voice answered, "Mrs. Mann, I do not know if you remember me. This is Otto Croenberg; may I have a moment of your time?"

Startled a little, she said, "Yes, Herr Croenberg, I do remember you. How may I help you?"

"First of all, I may be able to help you," Croenberg said. "Please accept my good wishes during what I know must be a difficult time for you. I would like, if you agree to it... to stop by for a few moments. I will not take much of your time, I assure you."

"Okay," Sarah said. "It can only be for a few minutes. I'm babysitting, is that alright with you?"

"That will be fine, I appreciate the time," Croenberg said. "Will thirty minutes be sufficient for you to notify the security detail watching over you?"

"Yes," she said. "What kind of vehicle should they expect?"

*****

After Otto Croenberg presented his credentials to the security agent sitting in an unmarked car at one end of the street, he was allowed to pass. Moments later, he rang the doorbell and Sarah answered.

"Mrs. Mann," Croenberg said. "Thank you again for taking time with me today. And yet again, my condolences to you."

"Thank you, Herr Croenberg," Sarah said, opening the door wide. "I took the liberty of making coffee; would you like a cup?" They went to the kitchen and she poured two cups then escorted Croenberg to the table so she could watch the children play through the window. "You are looking well, considering recent events," Otto said. "You remain as lovely as you were at our last meeting aboard that ship, the Paladin, so many years ago."

Sarah smiled. "Thank you. Now, how can I help you?"

"As I said, Mrs. Mann, it is my desire to help you, if possible, or as required," Croenberg said after a sip from the steaming cup. "I have learned of the recent events and they trouble me greatly. I hold your husband, Wolfgang, in the highest regard, as I do your ex-husband, Dr. Rourke."

"Thank you, I know they hold you in high regard as well."

Croenberg gave a slight nod of the head. "That pleases me. While our initial endeavors were... somewhat difficult, I feel we all have made progress and even could be friends."

Sarah said nothing.

Croenberg gave a slight cough. "To the point, Mrs. Mann. I would like to place myself at your personal service. Simply put, Sarah, I feel a moral obligation to both Wolfgang and John Rourke to... to the best of my limited abilities, offer you my protection in their absence... if you will accept it."

Sarah sat, unsure of what to say. Finally, she reached across the table and touched his arm, "Otto, I appreciate it very much. You are correct; these are difficult times for me. While my family wraps their arms around me in love, honestly, I feel as though I am alone. That is not their fault, it is mine."

Croenberg said, sadly, "I understand being alone. I have lost everything... but there is a difference from being alone and being lonely. I am comfortable with being alone; it is simply a physical condition. Lonely, however, that is a condition of the mind and soul and trust. John Rourke told me once not to trust anybody that was not... his term was, 'Old Blood.' I believe I understand his meaning."

Sarah smiled. "I have heard the term many times before."

"I do not wish to make you uncomfortable, nor do I mean anything inappropriate..." He let the term hang in the air. "I am simply offering you my friendship, my help for anything you may need. I feel that is an obligation I have to Wolfgang and John. If I had someone and I was in a similar situation, I feel they would offer the same thing to my loved ones."

Sarah nodded. "They would, Otto. That's just the way they are. But, you do not have anyone?"

Croenberg smiled. "No, not any longer and since that time, my life has never again presented me with that opportunity."

Sarah said, "I'm sorry for that, Otto, you are a good man. You deserve someone that will miss you."

Otto Croenberg smiled. "You are most gracious. Here is my card with my private number. I am sure Michael and Paul are more than competent and I mean no disrespect to either of them. Think of me as simply another alternative; another option. I am at your disposal," he said as he stood and walked to the door.

Opening the door for him, Sarah touched his arm, lightly. He turned to look at her. "Herr Croenberg, Otto... I appreciate and accept your offer. It is the kindest thing that has happened to me in these trying days." Croenberg smiled, then pulled himself erect, clicking his heels as if saluting.

"If you need me, I will be there for you," he said and left.

Sarah watched him walk down the drive and climb into his car. *What a strange man... what a dear, strange and lonely man,* she thought and then closed the door.

Chapter Fifty-Three

The phone call came late at night; for some reason... such phone calls always do. Sarah reached for the phone on the table next to her bed. Pausing but a second, as dread chilled her heart, she said, "Hello."

"First Lady, it is Helmut... Helmut Schmidt."

"Yes Helmut, I recognize your voice." Sarah closed her eyes and softly said into the phone, "Is this THAT phone call, my old friend?"

Schmidt took a deep breath. "Yes Fraulein, I am afraid it is. President Mann's body has just been recovered and I identified him myself. It is official and I requested the privilege of notifying you myself. I hope you are with your family and do not have to be alone at this time."

Tears filled her eyes. After several moments of silence, Schmidt said, "Mrs. Mann, are you alright?"

"I'm sorry Helmut, just adjusting... just adjusting to the news," Sarah said. Then she shook her head and refocused. "Helmut, I appreciate it was you that called. I'm sorry for both of us. I know that Wolf considered you a very dear friend, as I do. I will expect complete details and arrangements to be forwarded to my son and he will share them with me." Tears came again and she wiped her eyes. "Helmut, if you will pardon me. I must let the rest of my family know."

"No pardon is necessary. Sarah, I am at your disposal. I will see you soon, I'm sure."

Sarah broke the connection and sat on the edge of the bed, tears rolled down her face and she shook, but no sobs broke through her agony. Those would come though, she knew. Slowly, Sarah stood and turned toward the bedroom door. Annie was standing in it, her right hand clutched to her throat.

Sarah looked at her and the tears came again. "He's gone... he is finally and officially gone." There are times when there are no words that will help. When no gesture helps to heal. There is only silence and pain, this was such a moment.

Annie walked to her mother and wrapping her arms around her, guided her to the floor. They sat there, mother and daughter, but now the daughter was rocking her mother back and forth as sobs came, they both cried.

Chapter Fifty-Four

Michael's office released a press statement that called for prayers for the people of New Germany and the officials who "are working tirelessly to re-establish a government after this dastardly and cowardly attack." Two hours later, Michael himself went on television to read a message from Sarah. It said, "My dear people, today our hearts are broken and nothing will ever put them back together again. A great man is gone. He was my friend as he was yours. He was my husband, my strength, my peace and protector. Now, I ask you to do as I must. Remember him, cherish him... we have all lost much this day. Guard him until I return and then join me as we lay him in the peaceful embrace of our hearts and our country. I will see you as soon as possible."

*****

Before he left for New Germany, Michael Rourke was asked to make a presentation to Congress. Part of that presentation dealt with the State of the Union. "I have been asked if war approaches us again. Does the attack in New Germany, and the unrest around the world, herald more devastation? I do not know, what I do know is what John Stuart Mill said, 'War is an ugly thing, but not the ugliest of things. The decayed and degraded state of moral and patriotic feeling which thinks that nothing is worth war is much worse. The person who has nothing for which he is willing to fight, nothing which is more important than his own personal safety, is a miserable creature and has no chance of being free unless made and kept so by the exertions of better men than himself.'

"George MacDonald Fraser once said, 'The two pillars of 'political correctness' are: a) willful ignorance, and b) a steadfast refusal to face the truth.' I will not stand as one 'having no chance of being free unless made so and kept so by exertions of better men than me.' Winning or losing, I had rather stand with the man in the arena described by President Theodore Roosevelt when he wrote":

'It is not the critic who counts; not the man who points out how the strong man stumbles, or where the doer of deeds could have done them better. The credit belongs to the man who is actually in the arena, whose face is marred by dust and sweat and blood; who strives valiantly; who errs, who comes short again and again, because there is no effort without error and shortcoming; but who does actually strive to do the deeds; who knows great enthusiasms, the great devotions; who spends himself in a worthy cause; who at the best knows in the end the triumph of high achievement, and who at the worst, if he fails, at least fails while daring greatly, so that his place shall never be with those cold and timid souls who neither know victory nor defeat.'

"President Roosevelt and I would not have been political allies, he was a Progressive in the truest sense of the word... and I am not. Having said that, some of his words impress me more than did some of his actions. We are tired, my fellow Americans, but again to quote Roosevelt, 'Courage is not having the strength to go on; it is going on when you don't have the strength.' He declared there were all kinds of things he was afraid of at first, ranging from grizzly bears to 'mean' horses and gunfighters; but by acting as if he was not afraid... gradually he ceased to be afraid."

"Through his own strength and efforts, he preferred running the risk of 'wearing out rather than rusting out.' He said he had not led an easy life and he had never in his life envied a human being who led an easy life. But he also said he had 'envied a great many people who led difficult lives and led them well.' We have difficult lives and times ahead

of us. Lead yours well; you will find that, in and of itself, will be sufficient."

The press and the public lauded it as his best speech ever.

Chapter Fifty-Five

The flight seemed to take forever. When at last they landed, Sarah walked down the steps from Michael's plane. A band was playing a soft, funeral march. Helmut Schmidt waited at the foot of the steps. He walked to her and saluted, Sarah reached out her hand. Helmut shook it and stepped forward, he held out his arms and Sarah, with great dignity, embraced him. He escorted her to the limousine. Emma and her children sat next to Sarah and Helmut Schmidt, who insisted on holding Emma's baby. Michael's presidential limo had been off loaded and he, Natalia, Paul and Annie, along with their children, followed in it.

The drive to the funerary took slightly less than an hour. Black bunting was hung from windows, draped across store fronts along the way and the streets were almost empty. When they arrived, Michael took Sarah's left arm and Helmut Schmidt positioned himself on her right; the three walked slowly, somberly inside the cathedral followed by the rest of the Rourke family.

When everyone was seated, Michael walked to the podium to give the eulogy. "Today we lay to rest a good man, a good friend, a loving husband and loving grandfather... He was the president of your country but he was much, much more to us. He loved freedom, he fought for it.

"'For those who fought for it, freedom has a taste the protected will never know.' This quote has been attributed to a gentleman named Willie 'Bo' Nelson, of Mancelona, Maine, but some say General George Patton said it and I really don't know for sure. But I do know that Wolfgang Mann believed in it. If neither Mr. Nelson nor General Patton used it first, the author may well have been a Marine or a soldier, sailor or airman, but no one seems to know for sure.

"I've also heard that it dates to World War II, when it was first found on the back of a c-ration can in the Pacific theater of combat. Since then many have claimed it as their own, and have used it for different reasons. I will use it today. I know more than anything else, it was inscribed in Wolfgang's heart.

"Today, I ask you to join me in remembering the life he lived. He lived it with honor, compassion, dignity and courage. We will all miss him, but we should be grateful that for a while, a moment in time... he graced us with his presence, motivated us with his vision, held us in his love. It will be a while before a man such as he passes this way again."

Michael passed by the coffin on his way back to his family, laying his hand on it, he said, softly, "Goodbye my old friend. God speed."

*****

Soon, but not soon enough, it was over. Wolfgang Mann, President of New Germany, was laid to rest with full honors. The crowds dwindled and left, the news vans departed and soon it was just them. The security detail had strict instructions to remain vigilant but discreet.

Finally, walking back from the gravesite, Helmut Schmidt addressed the family: "He died bravely. He survived the first round of the attack at least. No one will ever know exactly when he died, but I assure you, it was both quick and merciful. We found him under a collapsed wall; we surmise he was trying to pull or drag the Vice President to safety. He still had hold of his hand. He died a hero."

Sarah said softly, "He lived as a hero also, Helmut. You did not know him in those old days. We did. He fought..." She had a soft smile and gentle laugh. "He fought well, he loved better. He was the gentlest man I ever knew. Gentleness wrapped around the heart of a fighter."

Chapter Fifty-Six

Sarah would stay in New Germany "for awhile," she said. Now, the rest of the Rourke family was on the way back to Hawaii. Seated in the conference room of the plane, while the kids enjoyed a movie in the back, Michael looked at his family with concern. "World events are starting to unravel and we had those sixteen years of peace before the arrival of the KI. Sixteen years during which our children were born into a world we thought had 'grown up' enough and we could start new lives."

Paul said, "And they were good years, it seemed as though we had lived through the worst and all of us came through it."

Michael nodded. "It did."

Annie said, "This kidnapping really shook my universe Michael. Now, Dad's missing and Wolf is gone and it seems like the world is starting to go crazy again. It almost feels like the old days."

Michael nodded. "That's the way it feels to me too, Sis. Do you remember when we went into our first long sleep after the Night of the War?"

"Some of it," Annie said, thoughtfully. "But I was younger than you."

Michael smiled. "Natalia and Paul remember it better; after all, they are the oldest."

Natalia leaned over and playfully hit Michael's arm. "Watch it Mr. President, remember you married an older woman."

Paul laughed and said, "Yeah, remember to respect your elders."

Michael grinned. "Tell me what you two remember about before the sleep."

Paul grew serious. "They weren't good times. They were hard and dangerous. John, Natalia and I spent a lot of time trying to find you and Annie and Sarah. When we finally did, the joy was short lived because the world was about to end."

Natalia said, "The world was so different, we were so different..."

"Exactly," Michael said. "Annie and I were kids; we had one chance to survive, thanks to Dad's planning ahead. What happened when the rest of you woke up?"

Paul said, "First there was the big surprise that you and Annie had been awakened by John, you were all grown up." He placed his hand on Annie's knee and squeezed. "That was lucky for me." Annie smiled.

Natalia smiled. "It was lucky for me too." She glanced at Michael, he was looking at her.

"Me too, best thing that ever happened to me," Michael said. Emma sat quietly; she hadn't even been born then.

Michael continued, "Dad woke us up and trained us. Teaching us those things we would need to know. After a while, he went back to sleep and Annie and I kept practicing those skills and growing."

Annie said, "Those were good days, lonely days... Michael. Those I remember well."

Michael smiled. "Then there came the second sleep. Mom and Dad were hurt, and Wolfgang decided to go into the sleep with them."

"He loved your mother even then," Natalia said.

Michael nodded. "Second sleep... second awakening... more problems... more battles until finally it was over. We had made it. Then the sixteen years of peace. Our children were born; Emma had become part of the family." He smiled at Emma and she smiled back.

"It has been the best time of my life," Emma said. "Until all of this got started up again."

Michael could see the pain in her eyes, the wondering... Would John Rourke come back to her? "That brings us to this meeting," he said. "I worry about our kids; they have grown up in a different world than you and I did, Annie. A different world than Paul and Natalia grew up in. Now that world is starting to shift and I'm concerned about their abilities to survive in this new world."

Paul nodded. "Frankly, Michael, I am too. We had that shoot out at my house when the Russians held me hostage and John Michael was hiding in the garage attic. Now, the kidnapping... And now Wolfgang has been murdered." He looked at his brother-in-law, the President of America. "Okay, shoot your idea; I think I can see where this might be going."

Michael nodded. "I think we need to focus on educating our kids, training them, preparing them. They have heard our stories, but our 'training' of them has been mostly camping trips. They don't have the skills that I fear they're going to need."

Emma said, "What kid does... if you're correct that the threats are increasing, very few children of their ages are equipped for it."

Michael said, "That Emma is exactly my point. We, we parents, are responsible to ensure our kids have the best chance for survival. Right now, I don't think they do."

Paul said, "So, what is your plan, Michael?"

"To get them that training," Michael said. "To immerse them... safely... but immerse them in a training regimen to give them those skills, continue their education but prepare them for what COULD and probably will happen. I'm thinking Dad's pet project is what they need."

Natalia spoke up, "He's talking about the John Thomas Rourke Survival Academy."

Emma understood, she said, "During the peaceful years, John worked on the Academy. He wanted a place where a person could learn how to take care of themselves in an emergency. A place where extreme skills could be learned in a safe environment. It took him eight years to get the training curriculum set up and implemented."

Annie said, "But what about their education, like the other things Dad taught us, such as philosophy, chemistry, mathematics and literature? He gave us an appreciation of academic as well as physical skills."

Michael nodded. "And we need to do the same for our kids. Here's what I'm talking about. Let's say we call it a Prep School, part of it physical skills, woodcraft, emergency medicine, survival skills. The other part academic, soft and hard sciences, all of this leading to a college degree."

Paul frowned. "The Academy can't do all of that, though."

"No, it can't," Michael agreed. "We divide their time between the Academy and Mid-Wake University. They alternate between both campuses, full-time... just like a college semester."

Emma said, "Paula's already doing part of that now. The biggest issue is when would they come home? I don't want to send the kids off for a few years and they come back all grown up. That's what Sarah struggled with."

Michael said, "They won't, they'll train, they'll study and just like in any other Prep School, schedules for coming home are part of the curriculum."

"What about their security?" Paul asked.

"While they are at the Academy, Secret Service agents will go through the training with them. The same team will act as an obtrusive security detail when they go to Mid-Wake," Michael said. "If you agree to this, I can have it set up within a week or two."

"There is another part of this plan," Michael said, growing serious. "If I am correct and the world is starting to unravel, the five of us are going to be busy with our own activities. We can't drag our kids into gun battles like we all went through. They're not ready... yet."

Michael continued, "Here are the threats we can identify. Peter Vale is tied to the Democratic Republic of Germany in Europe, an International spy and provocateur. Neo-Nazis, to include those housed in South America that launched the attack on Bellevue, killed Wolfgang man. A bio-weapon in the form of a genetically engineered insect is spreading a more deadly form of the hantavirus. A perceived alliance between members of the KI, and what is possibly a rogue faction of the Russians. Lastly, the alien presence we now have proof of, but no idea what they want or what they are willing to do to get it."

"Now," Michael said, pacing the floor, "here are the resources we can identify. We have an ally in The Keeper that can help root out the rogue KI and identify the Russian. We have good intelligence to continue to track developments in the Neo-Nazi movement. We have launched the first phase of the extermination plan dealing with the bio hazard. We have a captured alien craft and now know how to find it. It is possible," he said, as he sat down, looking at each of them intently, "even probable that my father has been captured by the aliens, and if that is the case... and if he is still alive... he may be able to help us. At least help us to define the actual threats and refine our responses."

Chapter Fifty-Seven

Shaw opened the door and looked in to see that Delys was awake. Entering, he said, "Hey Beaux, good to see you're still with us. Any idea who gunned you down?"

Delys sipped water through a straw and grimaced with pain. "No idea, Tim. Could be a disgruntled husband or someone from one of our old cases. After all, this is the first time I've been back in Hawaii since I retired. I've been rolling it around in my head the last hour, but... I really don't have a clue. You getting anything?"

Shaw shook his head. "No. I didn't see the shooter; shot came from across the street. Maybe a room window or roof shot, anyway... no witnesses that saw anything. We're checking traffic and surveillance cameras from the area. I was hoping you might have an idea." Delys shook his head.

"Right," Shaw said. "It was worth a try; if you do think of anything... let the orderly know to give me a call."

"I will and thanks Tim; I heard that if you hadn't plugged the hole... I'd have bled out at the scene."

Shaw shrugged. "You woulda done it for me. I'll keep you posted; I do have some questions that have been bothering me since the other night. If you feel up to it?" It was his turn to help a friend; he could tell Delys was hurting both physically and emotionally. Getting shot does that to a man.

Delys adjusted in the bed as Shaw pulled a chair closer to the bed and sat down. Delys nodded. "Fire away," as Shaw fumbled a notebook from his pocket.

Shaw looked at the notebook and said, "Do female frogs croak?"

"Huh?"

Shaw smiled. "You heard me, do female frogs croak?"

Delys smiled. "They do if you hold their little heads under water long enough."

Shaw nodded. "Okay, if you're going to make a parachute jump, at least how high should you be?"

Delys thought for a minute. "I don't really now but three days of steady drinking should do it."

Shaw stood up and flipped the notebook closed. "Alright, you're okay, I can see that. I'll check in on ya later. Oh, one more question, is it true a pea can last as long as 5,000 years?"

Delys flipped the covers back to show the catheter bag he was wearing. "Boy, right now, it sure seems that way sometimes."

Chapter Fifty-Eight

The family meeting was going into its second hour. After Michael had laid out the idea, Paul took over. Thirty minutes after it began, the first comment was from Michael's youngest, Sarah Ann. Forlornly, she looked first at her mother, Natalia, and then directed her attention at Michael. "But Daddy, I'm just a little girl."

Natalia said, "Sweetheart you are older than Aunt Annie was when the Night of the War came." That opened the door for a round table of discussion which lasted forty-five minutes, during which John and Emma's oldest son, Timothy, never spoke.

Paula had expressed concern because, "Mom, this is going to totally disrupt my life. I'm in school... I have friends... I have..." She stopped.

Timothy looked at John Michael and finally asked, "What do you think, Jack?"

John Michael thought for a moment before saying, "You know, it kinda scares me but, at the same time, it kinda excites me. I remember when the Russians tried to kidnap Dad; honestly, I was scared to death and didn't know what to do. When we were grabbed the other day, sure, I was scared... but more than anything, I think I was mad."

Tim said, "Yeah, it hit me the same way. I tried to stay calm but it scared me too. I haven't figured if I'm more scared or mad. I remember wishing I had paid better attention to some of the stuff Dad and Uncle Paul had tried to teach me. What do you think, Natalie?"

She stood up and paced before answering. "Yeah, I was scared also. I understand why you grownups want to do this but I'm sort of in the same place that Paula is. This is going to be a big change for all of us."

Emma raised her hand. "Here's my input. John and I talked about this several times over the years. He was convinced the world would eventually start spinning the other way and he wanted you guys to have some training and experience in how to handle that. Honestly, that's why he worked so hard to create the Survival Academy. Our thoughts, however, were to start you guys into the academy more as activities you could enjoy during the summer and winter breaks from school. Frankly, I'm not nuts about this either. I want my time with all of you, but I'll tell you... I'm scared to death for your safety."

"All of your lives, up till now, things have been pretty good. It was almost normal for you growing up. Normal except for the fact you were each part of the Rourke family. I know sometimes that was hard for you. I must admit, however, while I wish this plan was unnecessary... I think it is time. This isn't the way John and I had talked about doing it. But... Paul was almost kidnapped. Paula, you and Natalie, Tim and Jack... you were kidnapped and it was terrifying for all of us. I don't think we can wait any longer."

Michael stood up. "I remember Dad telling me, 'The wild-eyed criminal that strikes unexpectedly has always gotten people's attention. But it is the terrorist or criminal living next door quietly that appears normal before he strikes, which is the most pressing threat.' All of us grownups wanted you to grow up in a world that was safe and sane; not the kind of world we grew up in. While that truly was our loving hope for you, the realities of what has happened recently have convinced me it was rational, but impractical. We want you to be able to defend yourselves, protect yourselves."

He stopped for a moment. "You know, I told Dad one time that I thought my job was to raise John Paul and Sarah to be good people. You know what he told me? He said, 'Son, you are wrong. I used to think like you until I saw my first grandchild. Now, I know I was wrong most of my life. Your job is to raise them well enough that they can raise their children to be good people.'"

Chapter Fifty-Nine

"How ya doin', Beaux?" Shaw asked as he pushed to door open.

"Sore," came Delys' terse answer. "The main meds wore off last night after you were gone and I'm as sore as hell. They have me on a drip right now and that helps some. You getting anywhere on the shooter?"

Shaw shook his head. "Not yet. Have you thought of anyone who might want you dead?"

Delys smiled. "Only the ex-wife. I have thought about it a lot since your last visit, but I still don't have a clue. I have a question for you though."

"Shoot."

Delys adjusted his position. "I was still on the heavy meds when you came in but I think you said the shot came from across the street, probably from a room window or roof. That tells me it had to be over a hundred yards and an elevated shot. Correct?"

"That's what we think, maybe up to two hundred yards; and from the looks of your wound, the shooter was probably in an elevated position."

Delys took a breath, wincing from pain. "What if I wasn't the target? You and I were both moving when I got shot. What if they were aiming at you and got me by mistake?"

"Hmmm," was all Shaw said.

"Two-hundred yard elevated shot at night, on a moving target... Unless the shooter was a pro or a trained sniper... It wouldn't have been that hard to miss you and hit me. Besides, to the best of my knowledge, I don't have any enemies in Hawaii, some in Louisiana, sure. But if they wanted to shoot me, they'd do it in Baton Rouge, not travel all the way over here to do it."

"Interesting, we'll open another line of investigation," Shaw said. "By the way, I was reading a magazine in the waiting room. Had some questions for patients recovering from anesthesia. You know, to kinda check their mental faculties. You up for them?"

Delys smelled a rat but smiled and said, "Go ahead."

Shaw pulled a magazine out of his back pocket and acted like he was finding the article. Finally he said, "Okay, you are off the medications but are having trouble going to sleep. Are you a man or a woman?"

Delys smiled. "That's probably what's keeping me awake."

Shaw, acting as though he was making a note on the page of the magazine, said, "Just three more quick ones, what do the phrases 'Do It,' 'I Can Help,' and 'I Can't Get Enough' have in common?"

"I don't know, but I've heard them coming from the apartment next to mine a few days ago."

Shaw continued, "There are two subjects considered not appropriate to discuss at a nudist camp. One is politics, what is the other?"

Delys thought and said, "That's an easy one, tape measures."

"Last one," Shaw said. "Why do chefs recommend pounding meat?"

Delys smiled. "Loneliness?"

Shaw folded the magazine, closed. "Very good, I can see you mental faculties are functioning as normal; in the sewer."

"Get outta here Shaw, I need my beauty rest," Delys said.

Shaw stood, replaced the chair and said over his shoulder as he went out the door, "Yeah, you damn sure do."

Delys grimaced and shouted a single word at the closed door, "Comedian."

*****

Listening to a news broadcast on his car radio, Tim Shaw heard the first rumble of what would prove to show problems within the Representative Party. "The Representative National Committee's executive committee voted today to censure Representative Committeeman, John Croker, and seek his resignation after he was linked to a racist article on social media.

"At the outset of the RNC's meeting near Texas, the Chairperson, Alice Mayweather, said the committeeman's 'history of harmful and offensive rhetoric' has no place in the party and also called for Representatives to explore disciplining him.

"Croker refused to resign a year ago after failing to criticize Neo-Nazis and other extremist groups, while purportedly saying that blacks and Jews are different and can't 'control themselves.' While his detractors say he must go, Croker asserts that he isn't racist, doesn't support a racist agenda and was quoted out of context."

Chapter Sixty

"General, the tests were successful, this craft is incredible," General Thorne reported to the Chief of Staff.

"I understand that you were able to leave Earth's atmosphere," Sullivan said. "How did it handle in space?"

"No difference that I could feel. You asked me if I could fly this thing; the answer is, absolutely."

"So... are you ready for weapons testing?"

Thorne frowned. "Yes, my only concern is whether or not it would be detectable by either the aliens or the KI. My sense is you don't want to tip our hand with either of them, correct?"

"Absolutely," Sullivan said. "I see no reason not to 'keep our cards close to the vest'; the aliens definitely don't need to know we have figured out their technology and frankly I have concerns about the KI. Our Intel shows definite communications between them and some unidentified, as yet, Russians. John Rourke believes the militant faction of the KI is in cahoots with them."

Thorne asked, "Rourke is still missing?"

"Yes."

Thorne nodded. "After I do the weapons test, I'd like to see if the craft is capable of back tracking its own flights. That might pinpoint where Rourke is being held."

"Excellent idea. Where do you expect to test the weapons?" Sullivan asked.

"I'm thinking the dark side of the moon," Thorne said. "If I open up the craft to full speed, it would be a relatively short flight, probably only a few hours. I have figured out how to fire the energy weapons; I can simply send the blast into space where it will eventually dissipate. If I try targeting something on the surface, I have concerns the detonations could be picked up by the KI and/or the aliens. My thought is, get behind the moon and fire into space in such a direction that the flow of energy remains hidden by the moon."

Sullivan nodded. "Okay, let me run some numbers with the NSA and speak to the President. Get a good night's sleep General. I expect that tomorrow morning you are going to be the first human to do a fly by around the moon, in a long time."

*****

"Mr. President, I appreciate your time on such short notice."

"General, you said this is important. Have you had any word on my father?"

"No, Sir. I want to speak with you about the alien craft we recovered. Our test pilot has completed testing of the craft's flight capabilities. He is ready to test the craft's weapons. The plan, if you approve it, will be to launch tomorrow morning. Even though he will be cloaked, he will leave Earth's atmosphere on a trajectory that SHOULD prevent detection by the KI. We don't know about the aliens. He'll fly to the back side of the moon for the actual test."

"He's going to fire on the moon?"

"No Sir, just send the energy blasts out in space on a trajectory that will use the moon itself as a shield. If successful that will mean neither the KI, nor hopefully the aliens, will be aware we have mastered the technology. We are using a communications system that is encrypted on both ends and at a frequency that is very difficult to intercept. We can monitor the flight the entire trip."

"Okay, that makes sense," Michael agreed. "I still have been unable to contact The Keeper, however. We shouldn't eliminate them, should we?"

Sullivan said, "But they don't have alien UFOs to our knowledge, I'm sticking with aliens. When the tests are completed, Thorne wants to see if the craft can find its way back to wherever the aliens are hiding on Earth. That very well could tell us where your father is being held. Since the attack at Mount Rushmore by alien UFOs, we have to assume they are holding him but we don't know where. If it works, the next step could be a possible rescue mission."

"You're saying the craft would have something similar to our GPS capabilities?"

Sullivan nodded. "We won't know for sure until he tries, but it is reasonable to assume that it does."

"You know what assuming does, don't you General?"

Sullivan grinned. "Yes Sir, it makes an ass outta you and me."

Michael asked, "How do you see a rescue going down?"

Sullivan pulled a small whiteboard out of its case and went around the President's desk. "First thing we have to do is locate where the alien base is hidden." He said, drawing a circle, "Logically, it should be some-where above the Arctic Circle and probably on North America, but we can't be sure. If we can pinpoint the area, we marshal our forces for an air drop and go in. But, let's not get ahead of ourselves. Before we do anything like that, we have to have at least a serious belief such an attack could work."

"And by work, you mean we rescue my father?"

Sullivan nodded. "Yes Sir. We want a rescue not a recovery."

Chapter Sixty-One

The creature had not moved; he now turned, looking directly at Rourke.

I... will... use... your... term... KI. It... is... they... who... began... war... it... is... they... who... attacked... your... people. I... used... genetic... material... from... travelers. That... is... accurate. My... first... attempt... failed... because... the... specimen... was... defective. I... corrected... the... deficiency. On... my... subsequent... attempts... my... emissaries... were... captured... by... the... KI... and... modified. When... my... emissaries... attacked... your... people... it... was... because... the... KI... not... I... instructed... them... to... do... so.

Rourke shook his head. "There are a couple of flaws with your explanation. I could go along with the Captain Dodd clone being... defective. I knew the original and he was defective, as you call it, in a number of areas. But when the Dodd clone attacked me and my wife in the Mediterranean, the KI had not returned yet. We knew nothing of them, had never heard of them, except in legends. If fact, it was not until after we discovered artifacts that we knew they even existed."

My... first... emissary... attacked... you... because... of... his... deficiency... he... felt... a... need... to... destroy... you. I... made... him... aware... the... KI... return... was... about... to... be... discovered. My... first... emissary... desired... to... murder... you... and... obtain... what... you... call... artifacts... in... order... to... make... first... contact... with... them... himself.

John Rourke nodded. "Yep, that sounds like Dodd, alright. But that doesn't explain the attack on the Capitol."

My... emissary... had... been... copied... and... copied... again. I... believed... it... was... possible... to... correct... his... deficiency. I... was...

not... correct. His... deficiency... infected... several... of... the... others. They... acted... not... in... accordance... with... my... instructions.

Rourke said, "They went 'off the reservation' on you. The original Dodd also had a core group of followers more loyal to him than humanity. Probably it was them you cloned and thought had been infected."

It... became... necessary... to... terminate... those... individuals. My... later... attempt... at... contact... failed... also. That... was... not... due... to... deficiencies... on... their... part... but... on... mine.

Chapter Sixty-Two

Thorne woke early, grabbed a light breakfast and headed over to the hanger to go over the flight plan one last time; it would be tricky at best. To remain undetected by the KI, whose forces were still in geosynchronous orbit above the South Pole, he must launch into space with the bulk of the Earth's mass between him and them. To avoid detection by the aliens, he must leap into space on the side of the earth opposite North America, then go like hell for the moon.

He studied the layout of coordinates with the Senior Flight Medical Officer and the Flight Coordinator. "Not only do I have to get to the moon, I have to hit these coordinates and fire the energy blasts along these specific paths and azimuths. Then I have to navigate back to Earth, and stay undetected through all of it."

"That is about the size of it, General. What do you think?" Dalton said.

Thorne turned a wry smile on Dalton. "I hope you Brainiacs know what the hell you're talking about, especially when it comes to fuel."

Dalton nodded with concern. "General, we've been over every inch of this craft. We have not detected an engine, in the conventional sense. Nor are we sure what the fuel is, we simply haven't found a power supply. The only thing that makes sense is it is powered by the mind of the pilot. We don't know how; that technology is light years ahead of ours. But it's the only thing that makes sense."

Thorne nodded. "Well, I sure hope this isn't going to be a one-way flight. I have been able to bring up flight data on every other system but that one." Thorne stood up. "Not but one way to find out for sure, I guess."

The flight coordinator checked his watch. "Twenty minutes to lift off."

Thorne looked and nodded. "Roger that." He walked from Flight Operations to the craft. He took his seat at the flight console and had his hands buckled into position. "Wait a minute, go ahead and take these straps off. I don't think I need them anymore. The seat belt harness has been sufficient to hold me in place and I think I have keeping my hands in place, mastered."

The Flight Technician looked at Dr. Dalton; Dalton nodded and said, "Do it, the General is on top of it." The straps were removed and the Flight Tech saluted and offered, "Good luck, Sir."

Thorne returned the salute. "Thanks, I'll need it."

The Flight Tech and Dalton exited the craft; the hatch hissed closed and locked. Thorne buckled his headset on, laid his hands on the control panel and activated the holographic heads up display by thinking, *Systems on. Cloak on.*

He spoke into his headset, "Research 1 to Tower, over."

"Go ahead, Research 1, over."

After a comm check, he said, "Research 1, requesting permission to launch."

"Stand by Research 1; we have one craft clearing the restriction flight path... Alright, Research 1. You have permission to launch."

"Research 1, Roger. Initiating lift off, over."

The craft lifted smoothly, pivoted silently on its axis and shot off; this time over the Pacific Ocean in a north-northwest flight plan. "Research 1. All systems operational; will be initiating atmospheric breakthrough in three, two, one." Thorne mentally increased the speed and changed the attitude of the craft, it shot almost straight up. "Research 1, atmospheric breakthrough complete, increasing speed to the target."

He left Earth behind and headed into the darkness; even at the speed he was traveling... it would take a while. His path was curved to intercept the moon since both Earth and the moon were moving along their own orbits. In a straight line from the center of the Earth to the center of the moon is 238,900 miles. But this distance varies over the course of the lunar orbit from a little over 200,000 miles at the perigee to over 250,000 miles at apogee. The curved nature of the flight path added to the distance Thorne would have to travel.

The Flight Coordinator had told him, "It is a multi-faceted issue, very complicated equations but the simple view is, we're not able to hit the moon where it is at the time of launch. We have to hit a point of where it will be at a specific time. It's like trying to hit a very, very fast-moving object from an object that starts out at zero miles per hour. The moon will be at an inclination far above the latitude of the launch center. And so we have to launch at a particular time in order to catch up to the moon from below.

"Think of it like this, we're accelerating a package from zero miles per hour to its orbital velocity of 17,500 per hour. Then following a curved path to intercept the moon. That's the way the old astronauts did it, it only took about eight and a half minutes for them to escape Earth's atmosphere, and it was a heck of a ride for the astronauts. This craft is completely different from the old style Saturn launch platforms, but the curved path will be pretty much the same. Your advantage is you will be able to visually track your progress and make on the spot corrections based on your speed."

An hour into the flight, Thorne recalled it had taken Apollo 11 three days, three hours and forty-nine minutes from launch, to land on the moon. His flight appeared like it was going to take less than eight hours. Thorne also was aware that, in fact, the term "dark side of the moon" was a misnomer. The sun does illuminate it, as was proven in 1959, when the Russians got photographs of the far side of the moon taken in full sunlight. These were published in an Atlas of the Moon in 1960. The reality is that the far side of the moon, because of the lunar rotation, is simply never seen from earth.

Chapter Sixty-Three

The Rourke children and their escorts arrived at the complex headquarters. The flight back to the continent had been tiring but not exhausting. A mixture of excitement for the new adventure was mixed with fear about what they were going to be taught, and how the teaching would be done; it had kept them thoughtful.

John Rourke had decided it would be physically impractical to have one site that would be called the Survival Academy. Instead, many satellite sites, each capable of specified training based on its own unique terrain and climate, were called for. He located the main headquarters here in what had once been called the Texas Panhandle.

The kids were standing in the parking lot with their luggage when they met the senior instructor, a large man in a light tan uniform.

"Welcome to the John Thomas Rourke Survival Academy, my name is Mr. Dickson."

"You're not military?" Tim asked.

Dickson said with a smile, "No son, we have some military instructors you will meet but they are 'on loan' to us for specific topic instruction. Now, your courses of study over the next several years will be progressional. That means we're going to start at the lowest level, build your skills and then move up through all of the levels culminating in your graduation.

"Basically, we will cover equipment care and selection, ration planning, using a campstove and a fire, staying warm and dry, navigation, map reading, compass use, campsite selection, sanitation and waste disposal, communication and, most importantly, judgment and decision-making skills.

"We will also train you in tolerance for adversity and uncertainty, maintaining a good work ethic, stepping up to challenges, to have physical and mental endurance, self-awareness and vision and action. This will be a hands-on, learn-by-doing approach to give you the skills you will need to be competent, responsible survivors. While wilderness skills are important, we also have to train for survival on the street.

"There's nothing quite like seeing the remote wilderness on your own two feet, carrying all your own gear on your back, while gaining the tools necessary to become a great leader in the backcountry and at home. Backpacking courses often have you hike three out of every four days. You'll travel in small hiking groups, so you have more opportunities to lead, make decisions, and map read as you move through the wilderness. Hiking days begin early; you'll cook your own meals, organize and pack your pack.

"Most courses are thirty days in length, and focus on technical traditional climbing skills in addition to camping and travel skills. You'll learn knots and rope handling, belaying, rappelling, protection placement and hazard evaluation while working on improving your movement over rock and potentially being the lead climber. To help you learn basic first aid skills you will go on personal day hikes.

"We will supply your equipment which for the basic course will be a knife, mug, sleeping bag and liner, sleeping mat, rucksack and liner, head torch, water bottle and all technical safety equipment. On completion of the course, you will receive the coveted John Thomas Rourke Fighting Bowie designed by John himself.

"Right now the cadre will get you settled in and your equipment issued. We will meet back up in the training room at 1400 hours so you can meet your course leaders and teammates and ensure you have all of the required items and equipment. Then you will be released until 0600 hours tomorrow morning.

"We will meet here at the Operations Center then and using 4x4 vehicles, we'll cross some pretty rugged terrain and move to the wilderness base camp up in the Palo Duro Canyon. There you will be issued a basic food ration and then we'll head straight into some basic survival skills training. I warn you, it will be a pretty active day, but for supper we're going to treat you to an Alpine style dinner."

From behind them, the kids heard someone approaching. Dickson said, "I would like to introduce your primary trainer for this week, Sandy Tempest." The kids looked at each other; they had expected a guy, a rough and tumble type. Instead, Sandy Tempest was female, about five feet, eight inches tall, with short graying hair and what appeared to be a somewhat grouchy disposition. "We call her Ma."

Tempest said, "Not what you expected, huh? That's okay; it's the usual response when I'm first introduced. And don't think them calling me Ma means I'm gonna be soft on you. I'll kick your butt if I have to. We'll just have to grow on each other, I guess. Alright, here is the schedule of training for this week. Day two starts with a field physical training session and a lesson in self-defense, self-preservation and primal instinctive training. Next, you will study wilderness navigation; learning how to find cardinal points and move without a map and compass across difficult terrain to the remote overnight site.

"There you learn shelter building then you get to build your own survival shelter. You'll find out during the night if it is warm. Did it keep you dry? Next you will be shown fire lighting, rescue signals, steam crossings, stalking and a workshop on improvised harnesses and knots. Finally, we finish the day with a night exercise and a lesson on Astro navigation.

"For day three, hopefully you'll wake up dry and warm, which will mean you built a good shelter! You'll need to use your new skills to make a fire from scratch, check the snare and drop lines. Hopefully, you learned those lessons well because what you caught, if anything, will be your 'wilderness' breakfast. Then will be time to learn how to cross difficult terrain. That morning is the mountain training section, it will be a full course in mountaineering skills to traverse, climb and descend mountainous terrain.

"Once you have the easy stuff down, it will be time to cross extreme ground by use of ropes. We'll use some hills northeast of us for climbing; scrambling, Tyrolean line traverse, classic abseil techniques, commando crawls, river runs and river bank jumps are all on the agenda. You will finish late that day and return to camp late in the day. That evening there will be lectures on wilderness/improvised first aid. You will finish with a briefing on a real life survival story. The rest of the evening is yours, to prepare for your time on the island.

"During the fourth and fifth days... Well, call these your final exercise. For the next thirty hours, you will move by foot, 4×4 land rover, and speed boat to the island. There you will climb, scramble, swim, wade, jump and crawl. Food and water? Who knows, let's just say you'll need to be putting all your new found skills to good use. Survival on the island is one thing, but we want to know if you have what it takes to self-rescue.

"Again you will need all your energy, courage and determination to get back to civilization. If you are successful, we'll have the final passing out parade and awarding of the Rourke Survival Academy certificates and knives. Now, let's go get your gear issued, get you settled in and," checking her watch, Tempest said, "yeah, we got time for your first weapons class. Alright, let's go..." She wheeled around and walked off, never looking to see if the kids were following her.

They were.

Chapter Sixty-Four

Terry Hickok, the weapons instructor, was tall and lean with a no nonsense air about him. He said, "Dr. Rourke insisted that all students get an orientation into the energy weapons our military uses, but we were to focus primarily on the old style projectile weapons he had used. He always said, 'Energy weapons are good, but I trust lead slugs better.' While we will go over weapon safety, that is not the focus of this lesson. I'm going to give you an orientation in surviving a gun fight. Here are the rules, remember this lesson and it will save your live. Rule one: Guns have only two enemies—rust and politicians. Number two: It's always better to be judged by twelve than carried by six. Number three: Cops carry guns to protect themselves… not you. The average response time of a .357 is 1400 feet per second.

"Rule four: Never let someone or something that threatens you get inside arm's length, and never say 'I've got a gun.' If you need to use deadly force, the first sound they should hear is the safety clicking off. Rule five: The most important rule in a gunfight is to always win—there is no such thing as a fair fight. Always Win!"

Tim raised his hand. "I'm a fair shot, but I'm not the greatest shot."

"We will improve your shooting. For right now, focus on making an attacker advance through a wall of bullets. Sure, you may get killed with your own gun, but make him beat you to death with it because it will be empty."

"How many bullets should we have with us?" Paula asked.

"As many as you are capable of carrying," Hickok said. "Even then it won't be enough but you can carry so much gear you can't move, then you die. In a gunfight, especially in the beginning, you fire out your weapon pretty quickly. REMEMBER, if you're not shooting, you should be loading. If you're not loading, you should be moving. Because if you're not shooting, loading or moving, you're dead."

Jack asked, "How do we know what to do?"

Hickok smiled. "We're going to teach you, but a lot of surviving a gun fight is experience. You folks don't have a lot so remember: in a life and death situation, do something ... it may be wrong but do something!"

Natalie said, "Kids at school say a person who carries a gun is paranoid."

"Nonsense," Hickok countered, "Nonsense! If you have a gun, what do you have to be paranoid about?"

"Are we supposed to holler stop or halt before we start shooting?" Tim asked.

Hickok shook his head. "The police do it. You won't here. Just remember, you can say STOP or any other word, but a large bore muzzle pointed at someone's head is pretty much a universal language. And if you have to shoot... shoot to kill. Never leave an enemy behind. If you have to shoot ... shoot to kill. In court... yours will be the only testimony. Remember, this course is not designed to save the planet, but you may be able to save yourself and your family."

"Now, let's get you introduced to the weapons you will be carrying. We'll not issue ammo for them today. You'll get that in the field when you need it."

Chapter Sixty-Five

Arin Ágústsson, the Icelandic cop who tried to kidnap Rourke, was being interviewed again; this time by FBI Special Agent, Hiram Ellis. "I told Mr. Shaw I was sent to make contact with John Rourke and advise him of a plot the Yfirlögregluþjónn discovered."

Ellis flipped back through his notes. "Yfirlögregluþjónn, that's the Chief Superintendent?"

She smiled and nodded. "The Chief Superintendent is a student of the Neo-Nazi movement. After Nazi Germany dragged the world through the World War II and then was defeated, the threat of Nazism did not die out. Although, after the fall of the Third Reich, for decades it was a discredited political philosophy that few could envision reviving; it resurfaced. By 1959, a former American who had been a Navy pilot in the Pacific theater created an Americanized Nazi uniform. He said America had made a tragic mistake by siding with the Allies instead of with Nazi Germany."

Ellis nodded. "You're talking about George Lincoln Rockwell, totally anti-Semitic; he praised Hitler as a visionary leader. It was he who introduced the next generation of Americans to Nazi theories of racial purity and biological determinism. Though his efforts were an abject failure, Neo-Nazism continued to spread."

"Yes," she said. "Rockwell's legacy consisted of three new concepts that were designed to make Nazism, a product of fascist thought synthesized through German cultural assumptions, palatable to Americans in the late twentieth century and beyond. He knew he had to redefine the 'white race' as more broadly defined than Nordic Aryan. He also embraced many concepts that the German Nazis marginalized. He defined 'white' as any person not 'a negro' or a Jew. It was he who created the slogan 'White Power' to represent the solidarity of white people in America."

Ellis said, "Okay, but that was a long time ago. When Rockwell died, the Neo-Nazi movement he left behind fragmented into splinter groups that looked much like Rockwell's ANP. Even after the Night of the War, Neo-Nazism did not die. Even now hate groups continue to proliferate during periods of economic distress and societal uncertainty. They were mostly dissidents from high unemployment groups and those who suffered the dissipation of blue collar jobs."

It was her turn to nod. "Correct but the Chief Superintendent has watched as swastikas, jackboots, stiff-armed salutes, racial violence, perversion of religion to justify genocide, and epithets screamed by haters against Jews, blacks, and gays frighten good people everywhere. Today the threat of Neo-Nazism in America is a global concern.

"He has identified that a fairly recent new group, New National So-cialist Movement, or NNSM, has quietly grown into the largest Neo-Nazi group in the world. Even having said that, the group has not man-aged to attract a large following. It has consistently maintained a mem-bership of several thousand members. However, those few are dedicated, committed followers often seen in their black fatigue-like clothing with NNSM insignia. At rallies the members, dressed in black pants and shirts, often carry banners or shields bearing the group's in-signia, which includes a swastika and the NNSM logo.

"Their ideology is simple: NNSM calls for a 'greater world' that will deny citizenship to Jews, non-whites, and homosexuals. Mostly young, NNSM includes racist skinheads with ties to various Klan groups, racist skinheads and other Neo-Nazi organizations. It is the most explicitly 'Nazi-like' Neo-Nazi groups, which emulate the Third Reich. It has a vaguely paramilitary structure, with military ranks for its members."

Ellis was quiet for a moment. "Typical, even predictable. Let's stay focused. Why was the Chief Superintend ready to have you kidnap Rourke? Because he was convinced the NNSM has a new financial backer, a man named Peter Vale, and they are now ready to increase attacks, increase violence; and that there is a direct threat against the Rourke family."

Chapter Sixty-Six

The news reports from around the globe were not encouraging. Dozens of terror suspects had been arrested in Spain, Mexico and Central America. A day later, Mexican authorities said that they halted a plot to attack police officers by mere hours. A Spanish federal magistrate told a news conference in Madrid that twenty-three had been detained in connection with an international plot, with another two arrested in Central America. He added that a dozen searches had led to the discovery of assault rifles and high explosives.

The Mexican news agency, El Periódico Nacional, said that Mexican police had moved against a suspected terrorist hideout in an eastern town. The ensuing firefight resulted in eight terror suspects dead and twelve more wounded and arrested. At the time, officials said the militant group targeted in the raid included some who had returned from the Democratic German Republic. Authorities had previously said over three hundred German citizens had been recruited to fight with NNSM; it is unclear how many were still active.

Authorities in Mexico said they were ready for more trouble and raised the national terror alert level from yellow to orange, the second-highest level.

Prime Minister Jose Mendez said, "The increase in the threat level is 'a choice for prudence'. There is no concrete or specific knowledge of new elements of threat. However, police arrested at least twelve more people in anti-terrorism raids in three towns around the capital. The prosecutor's office said that the raids were targeting people with links to NNSM; one gunman attacked a kosher supermarket claiming ties to the NNSM terror group."

Police officials earlier told The World Associated Press that they were seeking up to eight to ten potential accomplices. The authorities had identified one of the three gunmen who carried out a series of terror attacks that resulted in the deaths of seventeen people, as a member of NNSM.

Authorities in Central America and several other countries were looking for possible accomplices. The suspect's common-law wife is believed to have fled to the Democratic German Republic in Europe earlier this month.

Meanwhile, the World Associated Press reported that a train station had been closed and evacuated due to a bomb threat. A police official, who was not authorized to be publicly named, told the WAP that the station was closed "as a precaution," but would not give further details.

The same day, the New Germany police said that they had taken two men into custody on suspicion they were recruiting fighters and procuring equipment and funding for NNSM. The two were picked up in a series of raids involving the search of eleven residences by 250 police officers. Authorities said the raids were part of a months-long investigation into a small group of extremists. However, they also said there was no evidence the group was planning attacks outside of New Germany.

Those arrested included a twenty-six year-old man with German-French dual national citizenship who had just returned from fighting with the terrorist group in Mexico. New Germany authorities said they were looking into possible links between a man they arrested in a southern city for illegal trade in weapons. That man claimed he wanted to buy a car from the wife of the first suspect. That investigation continues.

During the search of his residence, indications of illegal weapons trading were found to include the new SMART grenade. Known officially as the SAGM or Small Arms Grenade Munitions, it is a new kind of grenade that can find an enemy hiding behind an object, a wall or other would-be cover and detonate on its own. This is next-generation enhanced grenade lethality.

A police spokesman said, "When enemies take positions behind, say, low mud walls, typical of battle environments like third world countries, or if someone hides behind something in an urban environment, they can avoid grenade rounds. In order to most effectively hit a target, soldiers require a direct line of sight with a rifle-mounted grenade launcher and standard grenade.

"Just like other 'smart' technology that can complete tasks without its user providing instructions, this smart grenade can find its target itself. When the SAGM is fired, the grenade will recognize its surroundings and the cover used by the enemy for concealment. It then detonates over the target.

"Essentially an air-bursting grenade, the SAGM more than doubles the lethality of the current 40 mm grenade against targets that are not directly in a soldier's line of sight. Using an SAGM, a soldier, or a terrorist, does not need to do any sort of pre-fire programming sequence. The soldier, or terrorist, just needs to accurately aim the weapon and fire. The smart grenade will take care of the rest.

"While in the air the SAGM will detect walls, without even relying on a range finder. After it passes the wall, the SAGM explodes itself in the air, above the target. The idea was to have a 40 mm low-velocity grenade that is compatible with the rifle-mounted grenade launchers currently in use by western forces.

"The grenade is designed to have three firing modes. The first is the airburst after it detects the cover where someone is concealed. The next is a default detonation, when it hits the target called 'point detonation.' The third mode is a self-destruct feature. This one is designed to decrease collateral damage and reduce unexploded ordnance left on the battlefield or urban combat zone."

Chapter Sixty-Seven

"Research 1, Honolulu, approaching black out, over."

"Roger, Research 1, stick to your schedule, expecting restored communications in one hour, over."

"Roger, will be on sch..." The moon was blocking radio communications. He would have no further contact until he moved from behind it. Thorne moved to the position where the bulk of the moon stood directly between him and earth and stopped, in a geosynchronous orbit. He thought, *Weapons system,* and a new display appeared. There were several choices available, not dissimilar from his heads-up display in a fight plane. But instead of an inventory of rockets and cannon munitions, he saw different categories; blast, burst, trickle.

Blast, one from nose, Thorne thought, and a single surge of green energy erupted from the nose of the craft and launched into space. Not sure how the alien craft would handle measurements, he thought, *Burst, one thousand yards off port,* another green surge launch. At what he assumed was the correct distance there was an explosion. Aloud, Thorne said, "Right, human clones had flown this, targeting had to be something the human mind could use." *Trickle, one thousand yards off starboard;* this time it was a small, less intense surge.

Thorne thought, *Weapons system off.* He decided that blast setting was for long range engagements; the burst reminded him of missiles being deployed and the trickle like cannon fire. For the next forty minutes, he "played" with energy bursts until he had more comfort with how to fire, how to target and how to move quickly from one munitions to another. He even was able to target small pieces of space debris in orbit around the moon; debris probably from meteor impacts on the surface that had been blasted into space.

He was actually getting good at it, when the alarm on his wrist watch beeped. He shut it off and thought, *Weapons system off.* He moved out of orbit for the trip home. As he cleared the edge of the moon, he spoke into his comm link, "Honolulu, Research 1, tests complete, headed home, over."

"Research 1, that's a roger; we have the light on for you. Over."

Thorne settled in for the trip back; he thought, *Scan.* No display appeared. Thorne frowned. *Track,* still no display. *Navigate,* a display appeared. Thorne studied the visual; he had the tracking from this flight, the one from the other day, and what looked like the tracking from when the craft landed during the battle at the Capitol, before it was discovered. Behind that was a flight track which showed a lift off from the Arctic region above what had been called Canada. "Honolulu, Research 1, over."

"Go ahead, 1, over."

"Please have Dr. Dalton standing by with his camera upon my landing, over."

"Roger that, Research 1, and Baker Baker is standing by also, over." Baker Baker was General Sullivan's call sign, it stood for Big Boss.

"Roger, Research 1, out."

Chapter Sixty-Eight

General Sullivan was waiting as Thorne and the alien craft touched down and was immediately moved inside a secure hanger. Entering the cockpit with Dr. Dalton, Sullivan asked, "Alright General, the tests went well?"

"Perfectly Sir, I'll give you a full report at the meeting, but yes. The tests went well. What I found is this ship has a very precise navigation system for maintaining route accuracy and target tracking at very high speeds. This has to be like the old Astro-inertial guidance system, or ANS, on the old SR-71 Black Birds. It's the closest comparable system I know of that can correct navigation errors with celestial observations.

"Before takeoff, the ship apparently does an automatic primary alignment, bringing the ANS's inertial components to a high degree of accuracy. The ship itself tracks its progress in relation to certain stars. This star tracker component apparently can see stars during both day and night, and continuously tracks a variety of stars as the aircraft's changing position. The engineers tell me it tracks a minimum of between fifty-six to sixty-one major and minor celestial points.

"These are stored in what we would call the Mission Data Recorder. You can automatically steer to preset destination points or you can locate and identify those preset points. I think this is what you're looking for, General. I found a flight track that showed a lift off from the Arctic region above what had been called Canada. I memorized the coordinates. I'll bet anything, this is the site of the alien's location and John Rourke. One thing bothers me, Sir."

Sullivan said, "What's that, General?"

"As near as I can tell, this data recorded only has information back to the launch when we captured the craft."

"I don't understand."

"Sir, this indicates to me that either the craft's flight history was scrubbed before that mission, or it never flew to Earth."

Sullivan frowned. "Then how the hell did it get here?"

Thorne took a deep breath. "Sir, if it didn't fly here under its own power, it had to be ferried on a larger ship, a mother ship if you will. I think that is what is at that location in the Arctic. Doc, did you bring the camera?"

Dalton held it up. "Okay," Thorne said, "start shooting when I tell you." Thorne placed his hands back on the control panel and thought a single word, *Navigate*. The image appeared. "Okay, Doc, take some pictures as I shift through this record."

Chapter Sixty-Nine

The Captain had sent for The Keeper, again escorted by armed guards, a process now standard whenever he left his quarters. He was ushered into the Captain's presence. "Welcome," the Captain said as he pointed to a bench behind a small table on which sat refreshments. "I trust you are well, old friend."

The Keeper nodded and sat down. "As well as circumstances allow."

The Captain nodded. "I fear I have some troubling news. John Rourke is missing." The Keeper nodded. "You are not surprised by this news?"

"I have felt for some time that John was in some kind of difficulty, I put the feeling under intuition."

The Captain frowned. "Intuition? You have had no contact with him?"

The Keeper smiled. "How could I? My travels are..." he paused and waved his hands at the guards. "My travels have been curtailed."

"Then," the Captain smiled and said, "I have good news, the travel restrictions are lifted. In fact, I wish to ask a favor of you."

"How may I serve you, Captain?"

The Captain said, "I wish you to return to the surface. I wish you to discover what has happened to our friend John Rourke. I, like you, am worried. I particularly would like to find out the details of his disappearance."

"Why not simply ask?" The Keeper asked with a smile.

"We have, but his son, the President, has not been... forthcoming."

The Keeper said, "Possibly, he is worried about his father or he may not know."

"I am sure that is probably the case," the Captain waved it off. "But I want to ensure that our relations stay positive with our new friends. There may be a way we could be of assistance." The lie rolled easily off his lips. "You enjoy a friendship that our emissaries do not. He may be more forthcoming with you; plan to stay for several days. Take the time necessary to get the information I seek. Please gather your necessities; your flight will leave in an hour."

The Captain turned; The Keeper was dismissed. The Captain looked over his shoulder as The Keeper left. "Give my best to our friends and upon your return... report directly to me."

The Keeper stopped and turned. "I take it I will be allowed the necessary freedom for travel on the surface, if that is necessary?"

The Captain smiled broadly. "Why of course old friend, I would not insult you by sending..." He paused, looking at the ceiling for a moment. "Sending something as onerous as a guard for a loyal member of the KI."

Chapter Seventy

The KI shuttle craft set down at the Honolulu Airport; KI emissaries met The Keeper. "Welcome Sir," the senior emissary said. "I am surprised to see you on the surface."

"No more than I am to be here." The Keeper smiled.

The emissary said, "We have contacted the President's staff and they have granted a high honor, in hoping you will share their hospitality at the Presidential mansion. That is acceptable?"

The Keeper nodded. "They have sent a vehicle for you," the emissary pointed as a black limousine pulled up. "If you would like to leave now, I will ensure your belongings are sent to you."

The Keeper nodded again and entered the vehicle. Michael Rourke and Tim Shaw were inside. The Keeper looked sternly at both as they drove off. Shaking his head and pointing to his own ears, he said, "Mr. President, I have just learned of your father's missing status. I wish him well." He pointed to his ears again.

Michael nodded. *There must be some sort of listening device on him*, he thought.

"Thank you for your well wishes, he will be glad to learn of your concern... when he returns," Michael said as his scribbled a note. "Are you tired, do you wish to rest for a while?" He handed the note to The Keeper, it said, "Listening device?"

The Keeper nodded. "You know, I believe that would be an excellent idea. I have found that lately, I tire easily. I have heard there is a small spa in the Executive Mansion. Would it be possible to take advantage of it? Travel, even short trips, has tended to wear on me more than usual lately; it may help my old muscles."

The rest of the drive, they discussed what would be properly called, the pleasantries... and nothing of significance. That would come later, when they would not be overheard.

Chapter Seventy-One

Upon arrival at the executive mansion, The Keeper rested in the guest room for thirty minutes before he was to be entertained by President and Mrs. Rourke. Michael had told Natalia that their guest was being monitored by listening devices, probably secreted on his body. During the brunch, The Keeper complained several times of stiffness in his back and legs. "I fear," he said, "that old age has finally made himself known to this body."

Natalia smiled. "Please feel free to take advantage of our spa, particularly the hot tub. I find it most relaxing and it does wonders for muscle aches and soreness." The Keeper pledged he would and thanked Natalia.

Returning to his room, he found his single travel bag had been placed on the luggage rack next to the bed. In the bathroom, he found and donned a swim suit, then a luxurious long white bathrobe with the Presidential Seal on the left breast. Cushioned slippers completed his ensemble and shortly there was a knock at his door.

"Mr. President," The Keeper said when he opened the door. "I see you plan to join me in this wondrous contraption your wife offered. What did she call it again... oh, yes, a hot tub."

"Yes," Michael said. "As a matter of fact, I have found it helps my focus during long and difficult times. I have adjusted my schedule to allow for twenty minutes or so each day." Together they walked down the hall to the elevator that carried them downstairs to the gym and spa. Michael opened the door and pointed, "It is best, I have found, to start with a nice shower, it washes the grime of travel off and allows the hot tub to have more effect."

The Keeper nodded. "Thank you, I believe I shall."

When he exited the shower some twelve minutes later, Shaw ran a detection device over his head and body. "He's clean, no bugs here. If he had any on him they went down the drain with the water. My techs are checking his clothes and bag. They have already swept this area, you can talk safely."

The Keeper took the offered chair and Michael sat next to him. "It is good to see you again, it has been too long," Michael said.

"Things beyond my control have kept me away; has there been any word on your father?"

Michael shook his head. "No, but we are still investigating. It has been a most... difficult time for us."

The Keeper nodded. "And for the KI. Much has changed since our first meetings. Please convey my sympathies to your mother and family over the loss of President Mann. Yes, yes... these are difficult times for all of our peoples."

"Keeper, do you have any more information or insight into the relationship that has been built between the KI and some Russians."

"Some," he said. "I can confirm there is a relationship. I suspect it may be more complex than I initially thought."

"How so?"

"My sources have told me there are actually two separate factions within the Russians. One you know about and one I think is more secretive," The Keeper said. "There have been several communications and even flights between our fleet and the surface. We even have some Russian advisors on board our main ship."

Michael nodded. "We are aware of the advisors. What do you know about the communications or who they are from?"

"Very little," The Keeper said. "I haven't seen any of them, but there has been communications. I believe they are housed in some sort of hidden facility, possibly much like your Mid-Wake City."

"We think..." Michael began but stopped and looked at Shaw.

Shaw nodded and said, "Go ahead."

"We think we know where that second faction is and it is possible it's where my father is being held."

"I think that is not a good thing," The Keeper said with a frown. "I assume you are looking at some sort of rescue attempt?"

"Yes," Michael said. "But we need to know what to expect from the KI."

"As your father suggested, I have been observing," The Keeper said. "I have confirmed that the forces loyal to the Captain have been communicating with the Russians. There is an alliance there."

Chapter Seventy-Two

Michael Rourke, alone in his bedroom struggled; he had struggled with his decision since his father's disappearance. He was stuck on what his father had called, "the Horns of a Dilemma." He opened a drawer on the dark oaken dresser and removed a box; inside, a gift for his father. As long as he remembered, John had carried the A.G. Russell Black Chrome Sting 1A.

Lancer Corporation had crafted a new Sting especially for his father's upcoming birthday. The same double edge spear-point blade, but with green Micarta handle slabs, one side emblazoned with the JTR brand that matched the one on John's battered Zippo lighter and his fighting bowie knife. The words "The Survivalist," engraved on one cutting edge. The sheath was brown leather and also carried the brand and a spring belt clip.

Michael rolled the boot knife around in his hand, wondering, *Will I ever get to give this to you, Dad?* Sadly, he replaced the knife in its box, and the box in the drawer. *I will give it to you, Dad. One day.*

Michael knew he had difficult choices to make; either would be irrevocable, he would not be able to "half-step" this one. He remembered what his father had said once, a long time ago when he awoke Michael from the first sleep to train him and his sister, Annie.

"Son, when you are facing a dilemma, it is not important what you decide. The only thing that matters is what you decide about what you decided." His father had explained it this way, "Decision making is often difficult. Oh, it is not that bad when the options are vastly different. Do I accept a job that is everything I want, the money is good, the hours are short and I don't have to learn anything new? Or do I stay where I am, unhappy, underpaid, working long hours with no appreciation? Simple choice, right?

"In life I have learned about three decision-making processes. The first means that both alternatives are attractive to you, or you can deal realistically with your options head on. I have two choices, either of which is acceptable. This can also be called win/win. The second means both alternatives are bad and you probably shouldn't do either. Or do the one that creates the least trouble.

"The last is the one we most often deal with, both alternatives are attractive to you or that you can deal realistically with your options head on. I have two choices, either of which COULD be acceptable. But both call for doing something extremely difficult. The greatest difficulties are in the scenario that decisions have elements of BOTH winning and losing.

"In the end, one might be ahead of the other in tangible elements such as money or fringe benefits. But the other is ahead in intangibles, such as perceived honor, less stress, etc. These types of decisions form what have been called 'The Horns of a Dilemma.' Both decisions could be good. Both decisions could be bad. The end result is mostly left up to you and how you feel about the decision. That's why I say, 'When faced with difficult decisions remember this: It is not important what you decide, it is only important what you decide about what you decided.'"

Michael closed his thoughts. "Then I will make that decision," he said to himself. "If better or worse truly is my decision, I will decide that I will do the right thing." He walked to the closet and Michael Rourke, President of the United States, pulled out a large plastic container from the back of the closet. He dragged it over to an easy chair by the window and using a small pen knife, sliced away at the dark green "100 mile-an-hour" tape that ran around the corners of the top.

Lost in thought, he pulled out a pair of worn black pants. These he had worn bloused over the tops of shiny black combat boots. There was a black knit shirt that opened at the throat and a jacket of the same material as the pants. Next came a wide black leather belt, then a matching belt, with a gleaming black leather full flap holster. This is what he had carried his .44 Magnum revolver in, slung on his right hip.

This had been his "uniform" more than once in the "old days"; the days before he had accepted the presidency and forever changed his life. He thought, *Now, my uniform is usually a dark suit*, and he sighed. At the bottom of the box were several wooden cases; he pulled one and flipped the little brass latch with his thumbnail and opened the lid.

Inside was one of his two big .44 magnum Ruger Super Black Hawk revolvers. This, unlike its big brother, which had an eight and three-eight inch barrel and a scope, had no scope and a barrel length of only four and five-eighths inches. He thought about an old western song by Marty Robbins he had listened to as a child. It was called "Mr. Shorty." Aloud, Michael said, "... the .44 spoke and it said lead and smoke... and seventeen inches of flame." He smiled to himself.

He took the revolver from its fitted case, opened the side loading gate, pulled the hammer to half cock and spun the cylinder slowly with his trigger finger. Click, click, click, click, click, click... empty. He closed the loading gate, dropped the hammer and spun the big gun on his trigger finger as his father had taught him; slowly at first, then faster and faster. Forward roll, backward spin, road agent spin... he still remembered.

He pulled the hammer back to full cock, pointed the gun out the window and sighted down the barrel aiming at a small branch. Holding the hammer with his thumb, he squeezed gently on the trigger, riding the hammer down. The action was still buttery smooth but, as always, his father had been correct. The single action simply was not as good a choice for the way they lived.

He reached down again and pulled out the case with his Smith and Wesson Model 629s. Except for the barrel lengths—one six inch, the other four—the guns were identical. Each carried six shots of either .44 Magnum or .44 Special, both had a red ramp front sight and white outlined adjustable rear sight, both had large exposed hammers and satin stainless finish and black synthetic grips.

The next wooden case he pulled was even longer but not as heavy. Opening it, he pulled the handmade copy of Jack Crain's Life Support 1. He remembered the Icelander that had made it for him... Jon, he never could pronounce Jon's last name; he could see the man swim up out of the swarm of memories. He remembered the day Jon had given this knife to him. It was the day Michael buried his first wife, Madison, and their unborn child.

He unsnapped the retaining strap and pulled the knife out. He checked the nine inch blade edge in several places; still sharp and non-reflective due to its sand blasted finish. He checked the leather and the wrapping around the handle. He unscrewed the pummel cap and checked inside. The small plastic tube still held his emergency "essentials," the compass in the pummel cap... not a problem there. The whet rock was still in the sheath pouch; one side fine, the other coarse. He slid the blade back into the leather sheath and laid it on the floor.

Everything was still the same as it had always been... everything except, he realized... him. Again, through tears, he said aloud, "My father is missing and may be dead. My step-father has been murdered and his government all but wiped out. And here I sit; here I sit reading reports, watching the news..." He had made his decision; he reached back and picked up the case with his Smith .44s and pulled the shorter one out, pushed the thumb release and swung out the cylinder. Picking up one of the speedloaders, he dropped the shells into the chamber and closed and locked the cylinder. "No more..." he said to the room. "No more..." he shouted to the universe." Then he picked up the phone.

Chapter Seventy-Three

Dr. Fred Williams, head of the Mid-Wake Research Institute, rolled out of bed and grabbed the phone before it woke his wife.

"Dr. Williams, this is Michael Rourke."

Williams, not usually rattled, was. "Yes Sir, Mr. President. How can I be of service?"

Michael said, "First of all I apologize for the lateness of this call. I would not have interrupted your family celebration. Second, congratulations on your anniversary, it is convenient for me you decided to celebrate it in Honolulu."

"No problem, Mr. President," Williams said, as he found his glasses and put them on with his other hand. "I assume this is of the utmost importance, how can I help?"

"I'm sending a car to your hotel, Dr. Williams. It will bring you to the White House; I need you to meet with me. You were the first to speculate on the location of the unknown Russian base, you gave that information to my father before the Kamchatka operation. Can you bring your data and show it to me?"

"Ah, yes Sir, absolutely... give me a minute, please." Williams shook his wife awake, "Honey, I have an emergency call. I need you to get that old leather valise of mine out of the room safe."

"Excuse me Mr. President. I have that data here and I'll get dressed and be ready."

*****

By the time the car arrived, Williams was standing on his stoop. In one hand, he held the valise; the other held a stainless two-foot square equipment case. Coat and tie were in place, but one shirt tail wasn't tucked in all of the way. His hair was askew. The driver parked next to the curb and opened the right front passenger door from inside; Williams climbed in after putting the valise and case in the backseat.

"Dr. Williams, my name is Tim Shaw; I'm with the Secret Service. First of all, the President sincerely appreciates the inconvenience. Secondly, for right now, this meeting is strictly confidential. You may want to underscore that with you wife."

Williams nodded, pulled out his cell phone and called his wife. "Honey, this is one of 'those' situations. That's right, no one but you and I know about it and it has to stay that way."

Williams broke the connection, and nodded at Shaw. "It's handled." There wasn't another word spoken on the drive.

Chapter Seventy-Four

Shaw pulled into the private entrance of the White House; Michael was waiting for them.

"Dr. Williams, I appreciate this more than I can tell you. Did Mr. Shaw explain our need for secrecy?"

Williams gulped, his Adam's apple moving up and down. "He told me it was a secret situation, no further explanation was or is necessary, Mr. President."

Michael nodded and placing his arm around Williams' shoulder said, "Follow me." Moments later, they were in the private conference room. At the table sat Paul and Annie Rubenstein and Natalia Rourke. From the manner of their dress, Williams assumed he wasn't the only one rousted from a sound sleep. Tim Shaw poured two cups of coffee, offered one to Williams and sat down with his.

Michael said, "Doctor, I need you to go over the briefing you gave my father. The one about the secret Russian base, or what may be a secret Russian base. How did you find it, anyway?"

Williams said, "May I set up some equipment here?"

Rourke nodded and Paul stood up to help. "Do you need an extension cord?"

"I might, where's the nearest outlet?" Paul dropped down on one knee and flipped a cover on an outlet partially concealed in the carpet. "Excellent, no... this will do nicely." He opened the silver case, pulled out a larger than normal laptop computer and plugged the machine into the outlet. Turning, he opened the valise, pulled out several reports and a handful of computer disks. Turning, he asked the President, "Where do you want me to start?"

Michael said, "At the beginning, how did you make this discovery?"

"Honestly Sir, it was by accident. We were studying some interesting areas within Paleoarchaeology, specifically Paleomagnetic changes. While using a very complicated paleomagnetic model, which develops a record of past configurations of the geomagnetic field of the planet, I discovered an anomaly."

Paul raised his hand. "I don't think I'm following you."

Williams nodded and began again, "By using the paleomagnetic model, we can extrapolate spatial variations of the present geomagnetic field over the globe and time variations of the recent geomagnetic field. By those extrapolations we can find anomalies."

Shaw said, "I'm sorry Doc, but I don't understand a damn thing you just said."

Williams grinned. "Dr. Rourke said the same thing; let me explain. We look for fluctuations in the magnetic field over centuries, something that should not be there but the fluctuations say it is. The anomaly in question is located here in the Kuril-Kamchatka Trench beneath the Arctic Ice Cap."

Williams activated the large laptop and an image appeared on the screen. He turned around so the others could see and said, "It's right here. The trench extends for 3,400 kilometers from a triple junction in the west with the Ulakhan Fault and the northern end of the Kuril-Kamchatka Trench, to a junction with the northern end of the Queen Charlotte Fault system in the east. The Aleutian Trench is a convergent plate boundary. The trench forms part of the boundary between two tectonic plates.

"Right here," he said as he highlighted a point on the map. "Right here is what we believe to be your target. I believe we have discovered the location of a second and unknown Mid-Wake type facility they built back before the Night of the War. If I'm accurate, it could very well mean this is a secret base we've never known of. That could mean the

Russian threat is back; and I think, based on what your father intimated to me, things could well be complicated by a direct involvement with the KI."

Annie spoke up, "How big an area is this trench and how big do you think the secret base, if that is what it is, could be?"

Williams changed slides. "Here, the Kuril-Kamchatka Trench is over 34,000 feet deep and lies off the southeast coast of the Russian Kamchatka Peninsula. It runs parallel to the Kuril Island chain and meets the Japan Trench east of Hokkaido. It extends from a triple junction with the Ulakhan Fault and the Aleutian Trench near the Commander Islands, Russia, in the northeast, to the intersection with the Japan Trench in the southwest; an area of intense volcanism. How big? You can see this is a pretty large expanse of the Northwest Pacific Ocean."

Paul said, "How big do you think the secret base could be?"

Williams shook his head. "I can't say exactly but we know it is about twice the size of Mid-Wake." Shaw whistled quietly under his breath.

"Can you pinpoint the exact size and location for us?" Michael asked.

"If you can give me twenty-four hours and some dedicated computer and satellite time, yes Sir."

Michael sat silent for several minutes before he spoke. "Dr. Williams," he finally said. "Thank you for your time tonight, especially under the circumstances. Please convey my apologies again to your wife. Mr. Shaw will carry you home and on the way, I want the two of you to establish a checklist of what you are going to need. I promise, whatever it is, you will have.

"Mr. Shaw shall be your point of contact, your single point of contact on this," Michael said. "He will make arrangements for what you need and who you need to complete this analysis. This is a matter of the highest importance to me personally and to my family."

Williams nodded. "I understand, Sir. This will have my fullest attention." He stopped and turned, "Mr. President, we know where the Russian forces are, don't we?"

Michael looked up. "We do, Doctor, but we haven't been able to link telemetry together that says my father is at any of their locations... At least not the ones we know about."

Williams said, "Then if I am correct, you have found where your dad is being held."

"Thank you, Doctor." Michael stood and turned to Shaw. "Tim, will you get the good doctor home safely?" Looking around the table, he said, "I'd like the rest of you to stay for a while. There is something else I'd like to discuss with you." Natalia smiled, and Paul and Annie nodded.

Shaw stood and said, "Come on Doc, let's get you home before the cock crows."

*****

Michael went to the wall and pushed a hidden button; part of it pivoted to reveal a well-stocked liquor cabinet complete with glasses. Taking down a bottle of Seagram's, he poured a shot in each glass then returned to the conference table, two in each hand.

"You know for years, this was about all Dad drank," he said, passing the short glasses around. "I think it is appropriate that we have a Seagram's to salute those old days. As bad as they were, we were together through the thick and thin."

Paul looked at Annie, then back at his brother-in-law. "What's going on with you, Michael?"

Michael looked at Paul. "I've made some decisions that will affect the family, I think it is about time I tell you what I have been struggling with." Michael sat down; he unbuttoned his collar button and with one finger, snagged the tie loose. "There were several reasons I spoke to the family about the kids. Yes, the primary reason was I wanted them to go through some of the education that the world thrust on all of us. But there were other reasons, here they are," he said, taking a drink.

"First of all, the reports from around the world are showing a significant rise in terrorist activities, particularly the Neo-Nazis. I know of no better proof of this than the attack on Bellevue, which killed Wolfgang. I… actually me and all of my intelligence analysts, are convinced this was simply the first shot in this new war."

Paul shifted and took Annie's hand in his.

"Here's the way it shakes out," Michael said, slugging down the rest of the drink. "With the arrival of The Keeper, we have proof of a Russian conspiracy involving the militant sector of the KI under the command of the Captain."

Paul said, "I never did like that prick. How bad do you think it is?"

"We know…" Michael said. "We know there has been communications between the Russian forces and what we suspect is an unknown group. That's probably located in this anomaly Dr. Williams is investigating. We believe it is, in fact, a secret base of operations we have never known about."

Annie asked, "Natalia, did you ever hear anything about this before the Night of the War?"

Natalia shook her head. "To my knowledge there was only the underwater Russian city that we dealt with. But there was a lot of speculation about more Russian secret bases similar to our own Mid-Wake. After the war, in fact until just the last couple of days, I was convinced they were nothing more than pre-war jitters or propaganda. The current

Russian government has never made any claims or given any hints about something like this existing. In fact, they have gone out of their way to warm relations with us. I suppose it is possible they don't know about this new secret base; the records could have been lost during the war."

Paul said, "Are you seeing an involvement with the aliens? Crap, if they have aligned with both sides, the whole world is in danger."

Michael went back to the liquor cabinet and brought the bottle back, poured another drink for himself and left it for the others if they so desired. "Dad thought there was a link. In fact, he was convinced of it. I'm not sure about it. We have found coded messages that seem to be being related to the KI forces over Antarctica then bounced back to the earth, presumably to the Russians."

Michael looked tired as he leaned back putting his feet up on the conference table. "So far, we have not detected anything similar going on anywhere else. Of course," he said, taking a sip of the drink. "It is possible the aliens may actually be co-located with the Russians at that secret base. If they are... yeah, Paul. We have a real problem."

Annie sat quietly for a moment. "It doesn't feel right, Michael. The KI and the Russians... yes, that feels right. The aliens and the Russians... for some reason, that doesn't."

Michael smiled. "Doesn't to me either, maybe I do have some of your intuition, Sis."

Annie smiled. "Maybe so, same gene pool you know, big brother."

Natalia said, "Before we do anything, we have to know for sure."

Michael nodded. "I'm hoping Williams can get us the reasons, or... if nothing else, show us where we can ask more relevant questions. Right now everyone agrees this is not only our best chance... it may be our only one."

"Crap, here we go again," Paul said. "Russians, Neo-Nazis, more Russians and maybe aliens this time. Can't mankind get a break?"

"Mankind has caught a break, Paul," Michael said. "Us. Maybe the only break we will catch, but it might be enough."

"What are you thinking, Michael?" Paul looked at Michael, "What haven't you told us yet?"

"There are two more reasons I wanted the kids at the Academy," Michael said, after a pause. "The first reason is I wanted to be sure they were safe. The second is I wanted them out of the way for a while."

"Define, a while," Annie said.

"While we are busy trying to find Dad. I can't live with myself any longer just sitting here. He wouldn't leave us for others to go find and I can't leave him either. You know we used to make a hell of a team. I think we can be again, just smaller this time. Emma can't go, not now, with the baby. Mom... I think the best place for her is taking care of Emma and the baby."

Natalia asked, "Where do we look, Michael? Unless you have held something back from me... no one has an idea of where he disappeared to or if he's even alive."

"He's alive," Michael said with force. "I feel it and so do you, don't you Annie?"

Annie nodded. "Yes, he's alive."

"Here's what we know, as they were evacuating from Mount Rushmore, the attack came. Not by Russian ground troopers or planes or choppers..."

Paul nodded. "No, there is no questions the craft were alien. Sanderson's men reported seeing the attack."

"Exactly," Michael said, "and we don't have anything but suspicions about a Russian/alien alliance. Nothing."

Paul was silent for a long time before he spoke. "Are you saying that the aliens snatched John but not the way, or for the reasons, we have been thinking?" Michael nodded. "Then why did they grab him?"

"That I don't know. That needs to be the first question we ask them... when we find Dad."

"We're going to need some help on this," Annie said.

Natalia smiled. "For a limited period of time, we have access to anything and everything the U.S. Government has."

"For a limited period of time?" Paul said.

Michael looked at each of them in turn. "Yes, once we're sure we have Dad's location... I am resigning as President. I can't have the responsibilities of this office interfere with my responsibilities to my family or... my responsibilities to the whole of humanity. Dad never failed in his responsibilities and I won't either."

Chapter Seventy-Five

Croenberg dialed Philip Greene's private number. "Philip Greene, how may I help you?"

"I believe it is time for another meeting, Mr. Greene." Otto Croenberg, again in the persona of Darrel Johnson, arranged for a meeting time and location.

*****

A disguised Darrel Johnson sat across from Philip Greene. The restaurant was... seedy, not some place prone to the well-to-do. It was perfect.

Greene said, "Mr. Johnson, the world has changed."

"It has changed before." Johnson smiled. "Being able to initiate change without constructive direction is idiocy. The list of countries that have faded into history has often been the result of undirected, deconstructive change. The governments of the Netherlands, Poland, Switzerland, Latvia, Estonia, all the way to the Ukraine, don't exist. Their citizens now part of the surviving countries that still functioned.

"Other times, it is simply the result of natural catastrophes. After the Night of the War, what had been Scandinavia, Norway, Sweden, Finland and Denmark... well, they're locked under a mantel of ice along with what had been known as Northern Europe. Scotland and Northern Ireland are gone and the English government has been squeezed into the lower part of the island.

"Iceland continues to function only because of the volcanic vents that kept the ice-locked-island, warm in spots. Spain, Portugal, some of France and the Democratic German Republic, Italy, Greece, Israel and

Turkey are now the only functional governments on the north and eastern shores of the Mediterranean. Jordan, Syria, Iraq and Iran have become the Islamic Republic. Further east, India, Afghanistan, Turkistan and the other 'stans' have remained independent entities but their citizens have reverted to almost medieval existence. Change occurs all the time."

"Yes," Greene said. "But aren't WE directing the change this time. Aren't we making it happen and with a specific purpose in mind?"

Johnson smiled. "Mr. Greene, I need to be assured that your specific purpose is the same specific purpose of my principals. They want Neo-Nazism to finally attain its rightful place as the guardian and director of mankind. Is your goal the same?"

Greene started sweating. "Mr. Johnson, I thought the goal was to destroy the Rourke administration and let my party take over."

"And it shall." Johnson smiled. "It will take... certain manipulations and strategies for the final implementation of our plan. You will have your time in the spotlight... provided you understand the end game. You may participate in these manipulations and one of the strategies could include you. But Sir, understand, Progressives are only a tool for the Neo-Nazi movement. In the end, both parties will cease to exist unless guided by strong and dominant men like you who have sworn allegiance to us."

"But, what about Mr. Vale?"

"As I have hinted before," Johnson leaned closer, "my leaders have determined that after years of loyal service, Mr. Vale's... specific goals now have a more personal glint to them. He is working for self-interests above ours. I trust that is not the case with you, Mr. Greene."

"Why... why, heaven's no."

"Good Mr. Greene, very good. My Principals have decided it is time for Mr. Vale and his organization to... become inactive, if you understand my meaning?"

Greene blanched to a lighter shade. *He means they're going to kill Vale and all his operatives.*

Johnson continued, "But there is a slight problem. Vale has managed to create operatives across the world; operatives who we do not know. Operatives that must not be allowed after the..." Johnson smiled. "After the purge, if you will. You must help us identify them so they can be taken care of at the same time. When we strike, we must strike everywhere at the same time and eliminate even the scent of Vale's organization."

"But how can I help with that?"

"Why, Mr. Greene," Johnson said. "You already are. The valise at your feet contains some 'funds' you will donate to Mr. Vale, to assist his organization in their current efforts. We will track his activities and identify his hidden operatives and, when the time is right, eliminate all of them; and Mr. Vale at the same moment. Disloyalty and private agendas have no place with a true Neo-Nazi."

Greene nodded, thinking, *Crap, now I'm signing the death warrants for Vale and his men and, if I refuse, I've signed my own.* He leaned over to Johnson and whispered, "Heil Hitler?"

Johnson smiled. "Exactly Mr. Greene, Heil Hitler."

Chapter Seventy-Six

Former President of the United States, Arthur Hooks, was seated quietly in his library, staring at the tulip glass containing Cuvée Jean Godet cognac, grade VS deluxe. He swirled the Cognac, gently sniffed, then took a sip and held it in his mouth for a couple of seconds before swallowing. After a minute or so, he experienced the full range of flavors and aromas.

The aroma of expensive pipe tobacco was wafting through the air when his phone rang. "Hello?"

"Hello, Mr. President."

Hooks recognized the voice immediately. "Well, hello yourself, Mr. President," he said with a smile.

Michael said, "I understand that the gardenias are in full blossom." This was a code phrase he and Hooks had developed to initiate a private, secure and confidential meeting of extreme importance. A meeting too important to be discussed in any other manner.

Hooks leaned forward and took a pen from his desk set. "Yes, I have heard the same thing, particularly where there is plenty of water available. I plan to see them tomorrow evening."

Michael was silent for a moment. "I understand the weather may be better the day after."

Hooks said simply, "Well thank you for that information. Best wishes to your family."

"And to yours, Sir," Michael said and hung up.

*****

Arthur Hooks, dressed in old denim pants and a wind breaker, carried a fishing rod and reel as he walked along the beach. From time to time, he would cast a line, but he was not fishing. It took twenty minutes to arrive at the agreed upon location, but Hooks was positive he had not been followed.

He spotted another fisherman sitting on one of the boulders next to the bay and walked over. "I was surprised about the call, Michael," Hooks said as he sat down on the boulder next to him.

"I appreciate your time, Sir. There are some things I thought would be better to discuss in person."

Hooks nodded. "I see. Well our little game of code talking still works. What do you wish to discuss?" Over the next fifteen minutes, Michael laid out his dilemma, his fears, his quandary concerning his duty to the country and his duty to his family... finally he gave Hooks his decision on how he would proceed.

Hooks stood up and stretched; his mind racing. "You are sure about all of this?"

"Yes Sir, I am."

Hooks cupped his face in his hands and scrubbed away the confusion. "Michael, this is serious. This is deadly serious."

"I know, Sir, and there is not much time to prepare."

"No... no apparently there is not," Hooks said and sat back down. "Why are you telling me this?"

"Because you are going to have to help me prepare to transition our government," Michael said.

Hooks looked at him, startled. "What are you talking about Michael?"

"I'm resigning the presidency."

"What in the hell are you talking about? You're not through your first term. Michael, do you realize how hard a lot of people worked to get you elected?"

Michael nodded. "I do Sir, and none of them worked harder than you did. You have not only been my predecessor and mentor; you have been my friend. I felt you deserved to hear my decision in person."

Hooks shook his head. "Is it Natalia? Are you two having problems? Let Mavis talk to her, she can explain how hard it is sometimes for both the President and the First Lady."

"No Sir, it is not Natalia, but she does support my decision." Michael stood up and turned toward the former president. "Arthur, my father is missing. We don't know if he was captured by Russians or the aliens. The Neo-Nazi threat is spreading rapidly; we are seeing their influence here, sponsored by members of our own government. Now it appears that the KI and the Russians have aligned. My father is missing and I can't sit on my hands with a bunch of political busy work and wait on someone else to solve these problems, or find my father."

Hooks shook his head and walked to the water's edge. Reaching down he picked up a large pebble and rubbed the sand from it before skipping it across the still water. It hopped seven times; he turned back to Michael. "You know, my father taught me how to do that. Took him a whole summer, but I finally got it."

Michael nodded. "My dad taught me some things also, things I haven't forgotten. One of the things he taught me was to always plan ahead; that's what I'm trying to do now. Look, I have responsibilities in two separate areas of my life. I want to honor both of them but I can't. I have to pick one or the other and I have. But I don't want my personal decision to hurt the other. I need some help. I need some guidance to keep that from happening, which is why I'm telling you."

Hooks looked out at the bay for a long time, when he turned back to Michael he said, "Okay, I have some folks to meet with. Something like this can't be done over the phone, too easy for a leak. There is some planning and steps that have to be taken. Have you figured out what you will need to pull this off on your end?"

Michael nodded and pulled a folded piece of paper from his wind breaker. "Here's everything I will need. Everything, that is, except a truck load of luck; and Dad always said we Rourkes have to make our own luck."

Hooks nodded. "Yeah, and you folks always have. Tell me, how much time do I have to pull all of this together?"

Michael smiled. "Arthur, you have to tell me. As soon as you tell me everything is staged, I'll make the announcement. But I'm not talking about months or even weeks. I'm talking about days. I won't be able to do anything until I have the Intel and figure out what to do, where to do it and who to do it to. That's what is killing me right now, so please hurry."

Hooks nodded. "I will try but you have to understand... I have to not only look at your wishes, Michael. I have to look into the legality, our national security, hell, even our national image. This transition will have to be so tightly managed; we will have to plug gaps that don't even exist at this moment. And... we have to structure and manage for a future; a future that also doesn't exist yet."

Michael stood and extended his hand to Hooks. "My Dad always told me to focus on today; not on yesterday which is already gone, but plan for the tomorrow that isn't here yet."

Chapter Seventy-Seven

Otto Croenberg was no longer wearing the Darrel Johnson disguise as he sat with Paul Rubenstein. He said, "You are serious about this?"

Paul nodded. "Michael is. There will be a lot of moving parts to this Otto. Some of them... well they may belong to you. Sarah told me about your conversation with her. Thank you for that, it meant a lot to her. It means a lot to the rest of the family and if we can get John back, it will mean a lot to him."

Croenberg nodded. "I hope I was able to convey I meant no disrespect to you or Michael."

Paul smiled. "You did, have no concerns, and again, my family thanks you for the offer."

Croenberg said, "Honestly Paul, on one hand I want to go with you on this search..."

Paul stopped him. "Not this time, maybe another. Michael, Natalia, Annie and I discussed the possibility and we are in agreement. We need and want you here to watch not only over Sarah, but Emma and the baby. While your continued role as Darrel Johnson is a real probability... they need to be your primary focus."

Croenberg said solemnly, "I will guard them as if they were my own family. In a way they are. Plus, I don't want to have to deal with an angry Jew and the rest of the Rourke family if I fail." He smiled.

Paul smiled back. "Don't screw this up, you Nazi bastard." Then they shook hands.

Croenberg said, "I think it is time for me to have a conversation with the Aqrab."

*****

Tuviah Friedman sat across from Otto Croenberg, a situation he had not contemplated. After studying Croenberg, Tuviah asked, "Why are you telling me this, Herr Croenberg?"

Croenberg smiled. "You told Mr. Delys and Mr. Shaw that you work for an organization which hunts Nazis, more accurately Neo-Nazis. I believe it is called the Aqrab?"

Friedman nodded as he stoked the Meerschaum pipe to life. "Correct."

"You believed I was part of a plot to harm Paul Rubenstein, I am not." Friedman nodded again and Croenberg continued, "You also said that the Aqrab was not a 'well known entity' and you sought neither 'acknowledgement nor accolades.' The Aqrab concerns itself with beginnings and endings and focuses on protection, not necessarily of the individual but the essence of the Jewish people."

"Again Sir, you are correct."

Croenberg smiled. "Then Tuviah, I am giving you a gift. The beginning of the ending of the Neo-Nazi movement." Friedman's eyes widened for an instant but said nothing. "I have a man on the inside and a plan in motion, but it will require your people to complete it. It cannot be tied in any way to an individual; any individual. Are you interested?"

Tuviah Friedman stared at the former Neo-Nazi with a glare. "Why, Herr Croenberg, are you giving me this gift? What is in it for you?"

"A fair question, Tuviah." Croenberg sat back, thinking. "The answer is a simple one: my redemption."

Chapter Seventy-Eight

Fred Williams was tired, but excited. He and his team had been crunching data and numbers, and then they crunched them two more times. He was confident he had the answers his president needed. He made the call to Tim Shaw.

"Shaw."

"Mr. Shaw, this is Fred Williams."

"Hello Doc, how is it coming?"

"I think I have your answers. I think it is time to meet again."

"You sure?"

"I believe so, Mr. Shaw. We've been over the data enough; I'm willing to say, yes."

"I'll make the call then. Stay close to your phone and be ready to move when I call." Shaw broke the connection before Williams could answer.

Michael Rourke's new cell phone jingled. Shaw had insisted on a new, untraceable burn phone for conversations of this nature. "Hello," Michael said.

"The man with the magnetic personality wants to meet," Shaw said.

"Good news?"

"Seems like it," Shaw said. He could hear Michael take a deep breath and slowly release it.

"Excellent, same procedure and location as last time," Michael said. "Let me call the others. Call me back with the time and you handle transport like last time."

Shaw said, "Will do. He seems pretty excited Michael, this could be it."

"I'll have my fingers crossed," Michael said and broke the connection; he began calling the rest of the family.

*****

Natalia, assisted by several linguists who spoke and read Russian, was the first to find a clue. An obscure clue, but still a clue. Her team of linguists began to pour over the mass of data, yet again. She called Michael. "Hey, I think I have found something. What do you know about underwater habitats?"

"You mean like Mid-Wake?" he asked.

"Yes," she said.

"Not much," he said, thinking. "According to what we learned at Mid-Wake, when we first found it, underwater structures had been around for a long time, mostly for underwater research on marine environments. Most of the early ones lacked regenerative systems for air, water, food, electricity, and other resources. However, recently some new underwater habitats allow for these resources to be delivered using pipes, or generated within the habitat, rather than manually delivered."

"Correct," Natalia agreed. "They were also used to study the needs of human physiology and the physical environment." Things like pressure, temperature, light, humidity and toxins associated with living at depth. Research was devoted particularly to the physiological processes and limits of breathing gases under pressure, and astronaut training, as well as for research on marine ecosystems."

"If I'm remembering correctly, didn't the studies began in the early 1960s and were built by private individuals or governments?"

"Yes," she said. "The early ones were used almost exclusively for research and exploration, but there was at least one underwater habitat that had been provided for recreation and tourism."

"Okay, so what have you found?" He could hear her shuffling papers in the background.

"I know the Russians had one," she said. "But, I think I have evidence of another; I have found references to something called Gluboko Zvezda. In English that means Deep Star. It was built to study such things as microbes and how they develop when a person is injured and develops gas gangrene."

"What's that?"

"Bad stuff. There was an underwater habitat called La Chalupa that operated in Puerto Rico before the Night of the War and they had an accident," she explained. "During the habitat's second mission, a steel cable wrapped around one individual's left wrist, shattering his arm, which he subsequently lost to gas gangrene. Gas gangrene is most often caused by bacteria called clostridium perfringens. Clostridium is found nearly everywhere, but no one had studied the effects at great depths. The bacteria grows inside the body, it makes gas and harmful substances or toxins that can damage body tissues, cells, and blood vessels."

"Interesting, but I don't see the connection."

"Let me finish. Construction on Deep Star was begun in 1970s; it cost billions of dollars to build. In 1979, two years before the Night of the War, record keeping on the project was stopped and most purged from the Russian achieves. Our research indicates it was for more than some kind of underwater medical study. We found some of the old shipping records were missed in the purge, and dealt with supplies, construction and logistics. There are mentions of 'special packages'; that's how the Russian government referred to nuclear missiles."

Michael frowned. "Do you have an idea where it was?"

"Yes," she said. "The same trench where the anomaly is located, that seems pretty coincidental, don't you think?"

Michael was quiet for a moment. "Too coincidental, good work; now all we have to do is figure out how to pierce Deep Star's defense, gain entry and find my father and get out."

Chapter Seventy-Nine

The top secret Lockout Team conference was underway. Retired Captain Daniel Thomas Hasher, former head of operations at the Hopper Information Services Center, said, "Mr. President, allow me to say this operation is speculative. The evidence is circumstantial at best. I am not seeing what I would call actionable intelligence."

Michael said, "I understand Captain, the decision to move or not move on this is, however, mine. And I have made it."

Hasher nodded and began the briefing, "Sir, the Long-Term Reconnaissance and Combat System or LMRS drones, were designed to be torpedo tube-launched. Even the smaller LMRSs are equipped with both forward-looking and side-scan sonar. We'll use two of them to pinpoint the target."

"Captain, I haven't heard of this technology, is it new?" Michael asked.

"Not at all, Mr. President. It is just not well known out of the naval community. As naval requirements changed, we had to develop a primary underwater 'first strike' asset." He pushed a button and a new slide appeared on the screen. "The LMRS are the next generation of manned and unmanned underwater combat vehicles to be used in minefield reconnaissance, intelligence collection, trailing, tagging and deception. But we needed attack capabilities for potential future options, with command modalities that range from simple remote control to near-total autonomy."

Hasher changed slides on the big screen. "We also have Manned Underwater Vehicles. This one is the MANTA 6, our latest version. We are also sending ten of them as the main strike force. Each is sixty-five feet long and weighs fifty-five tons and carries a pilot, weapons officer and a squad of eight members of the 442nd. It is cramped but it can handle that many.

"These are like underwater battleships and carry a variety of full-scale weapons. MANTAs can launch heavyweight torpedoes against enemy ships, submarines, and even shore installations. They are large, somewhat ray-shaped vehicles, and each of the main battle submarines carries four MANTAs externally. Four thruster pods make this our most maneuverable craft.

"The propulsion systems for the smaller UUVs are similar but not as effective; the MANTAs use a vastly different system. In the last few years we have made progress in propulsion, control, hydrodynamics, and sensor technology as well as operating depth. For this mission we are deploying both MANTAs and UUVs in a coordinated attack system. The MANTAs will have radio control of the UUVs and direct their purpose or... their destruction as needed."

"Their destruction would be tied to using them as a weapon, I presume?" someone asked.

"Exactly," Hasher responded. "By using UUVs to complement the larger MANTAs, we can have a significant force-multiplier. They are simply a more cost-effective way of getting things done. They have enabled the development of more broadly capable vehicles and freed the imagination of naval planners to propose new and innovative operational applications for them. The UUVs are fifteen feet long and weigh in at about a thousand pounds.

"DARPA, the Defense Advanced Research Projects Agency, developed these vehicles to have a demonstrated range capability of sixty to one hundred nautical miles, at three to four knots, depending on payload, the most common of which has been side-scan sonar. They are powered by banks of upgraded alkaline-lithium cells and have demonstrated a mission range of slightly over fifteen hundred nautical miles.

"Each UUV carries a total of six underwater mini-torpedoes; three forward and three aft. The MANTAs, designated to provide cover for the operation, each will carry the same compliment of standard 'fish' but will also have a multidirectional energy burst cannon controlled by the pilot. Additionally, these cover craft will have programmable torpedo pods."

"So Captain, you think the rescue attempt will be successful?" Michael asked.

Hasher grew silent. "Mr. President, I can't make any promises. However, like you I don't see any other possibilities for finding your father. The discovery of this Deep Star anomaly is... it's the only lead we may have. None of our efforts have been able to locate him. Obviously, he is not being held at any location we are aware of."

Hasher cleared his throat. "Here are our limitations. We don't have enough information, number one. It is like he has disappeared from the face of the earth. Can I say for sure he is at Deep Star? No. But I can't say he is not, either. I think we can assume that the docking hatches on Deep Star are no different than those we use at Mid-Wake, although they will be configured for Russian subs. The ones for the MANTAs have been converted to those. If you can gain access to an air lock and dock, you can off load your penetration force and begin your search."

"Yeah, then all we have to do is find John Rourke and get out of Deep Star. What about communications?" Jason Darkwater, Michael's Vice President, asked.

Hasher said, "Yes, that's all you have to do. Communications remain a problem area, particularly to and from underwater vehicles at depth. Despite the availability of undersea acoustic communication techniques, in which 'channel-matching' and intensive digital signal processing are used to sort out multi-path interference in shallow water, effective data rates will likely be limited to no more than several tens of kilobits per second. Short-range acoustic communications have been used for exchanging data and command information among nearby vehicles and docking stations, or when operating close to manned host platforms.

"But because so much of the data that prospective long-range missions are intended to collect, are high-bandwidth-like imagery, electronic or communications intelligence, we will use a series of both submerged and surface buoys in contact with both GPS and communication satellites and as relays. Relatively short-range, two-way acoustic data links will establish connectivity between the vehicles and buoys for both data and command/control.

"Main communication to the operational command will be in the ELF or Extremely Low Frequency bands. That will help avoid detection prior to the attack. As you all know, ELF or sub radio frequencies have a variety of uses. Not the least of which is to communicate with submarines and other submerged targets."

Darkwater frowned. "Earlier you had said the KI fleet, and whomever they are communicating with, use our own satellite system to bounce or ricochet messages on a frequency of zero to three hundred Hertz."

Hasher nodded. "As you know from your time in the Navy, Sir, it is not only what we use to communicate with our submersed ships, it is the exact system that was used by the old Soviet/Russian Navy using SIASs or Submarine Integrated Antenna Systems."

"Mr. President," Hasher said solemnly. "We have been unable to find and track the flight patterns of the alien craft that took your father. It entered a storm front as it crossed into Canada. We lost it. This is not a strong lead, it simply is the only one we have at the moment. The investigation is continuing and if we find another possible location... we can develop an attack plan for it. Right now, this is the only possibility I see. Do we go?"

Michael said simply, "We go. Vice President Darkwater, you will assume leadership while I'm gone. Is the cover story, explaining my absence, ready?"

Darkwater nodded. "Pretty much the same story as the last time. We've set up a wing at Tripler Medical Center; part of the staff that removed the tattoos from Kuriname's people will be used for the cover. I will again temporarily assume the presidency as called for by law when the President is not able to fulfill the office because of medical conditions. We will fake your entry tomorrow and release the story. I'm sure there will be a lot of speculation but we're on top of it."

Michael nodded. "Thank you. I give you my word, this is the last time we will do this."

Chapter Eighty

The MANTA force was divided into two teams of five craft each. Call signs were by team color and sequential numbers: one, two, etc. CWO Wes Sanderson commanded Blue Team, his call sign–Blue One. Akiro Kuriname commanded Red Team, call sign–Red One. Red One and Blue One would be the primary penetration teams, with Red and Blue Two held in reserve until needed. The remaining ships would "fly cover" during the penetration attempt of the Deep Star.

Sanderson's ship was piloted by Chief Petty Officer, David Reynolds, a combat veteran and one of the chief instructors at the MANTA facility. Five feet, eight inches tall, Reynolds had dark stubble growing on his head and beard line, and sky blue eyes often described by the ladies as "stunning." Thirty years old and recently divorced, Reynolds was the best pilot in the MANTA fleet.

Reynolds' number two instructor at MANTA, CPO Byron Flores, was Kuriname's pilot. Flores, a mix of Hispanic and Scottish ancestry, was light skinned with short, flaming red stubble hair and clean shaven. Married with two daughters, Flores was simply called "Pop" around the facility. This was his last mission; after retirement Pop and his family were starting a small farm in southwestern Missouri.

Squeezed into the cargo compartment, along with eight of Sanderson's men, was Michael Rourke. Each wore the latest version of the underwater winged dive suit and hemosponges. However, at these depths, they would be useless in free diving but could prove useful in any flooded areas of the Deep Star; provided these did not open out into the Trench itself. The pressures were simply too great; if a MANTA was hit and the hull breached... it was a death sentence.

Each Dog Soldier carried both an energy rifle and pistol; Michael had insisted that each also carry backup, high-capacity conventional handguns. Satchel charges, smoke grenades, flash-bangs and extra ammo hung from every assault vest along with medical kits. They had to be as self-sustaining as possible.

With their combat regalia, weapons, etc., they couldn't cram ten soldiers in the compartment of any of the MANTAs. The penetration teams would be sixteen people strong. If anyone was injured, help would not be coming to them. Serious injuries meant a trip back to the surface... if they could.

If they couldn't, they were stuck at a depth of over 34,000 thousand feet and pressures near to 15,000 pounds per square inch.

Chapter Eighty-One

The MANTAs, UUVs and reconnaissance drones were ferried to each end of the Trench; Red Team at the southeast corner, close to the Kamchatka Peninsula, Blue Team at the eastern end near Hokkaido, Japan. Once the MANTAS carried into position by Mid-Wake submarines, were launched they took up station at a depth of 300 feet. The MANTAs, UUVs and drones wore stealth, radar-defeating covering.

Communications buoys were air dropped. Their small containers broke open when they hit the surface of the water, and the buoys were released and began sinking to their proper depths. Total flight time over the area for the VTOL transport ships was less than thirty seconds and their flight paths never varied. Anyone monitoring their radar signatures would have not been aware anything had occurred.

Reynolds and Flores established communications control with their unmanned vehicles first, then with each other, and then the two forces submerged still deeper and moved closer to their staging point. They resembled large, swimming schools of fish being led by gigantic sting rays. On arrival at their stations, Reynolds and Flores sent their recon drones down to depth and monitored their progress on view screens at their pilot consoles. Aided by ocean currents, Red Team's drone traveled slightly faster than Blue Team's as the drones swept with front sonar for guidance, and side sonar and cameras for details of the Trench walls. Other sensors searched for indications of radio waves or electrical energy.

The Red Team drone had passed the halfway mark and was approaching the Blue Team drone when the first alarms beeped on the pilot's consoles. Flores told Kuriname, "We're getting something, heads up. Watch the screens." Kuriname focused on the visuals, allowing Flores to monitor the sensor readings.

"I'm getting something on the south wall," Kuriname said. "Getting closer but I still can't make it out. Wait a minute!" he shouted. "There it is, mark the location on GPS. That is definitely man-made. It is amazing they were able to build at this depth."

Flores shook his head. "I think they must have pre-assembled the structures, sank them to where they wanted them, then anchored them on the floor mechanically. Hold on, Blue Team's drone is coming by ours... no, that's good, about ten meters of difference between their depths. Wanted to be sure they didn't smack into each other. Okay, I have a visual on the Blue drone... here it comes."

Kuriname added, "And there it goes. Any activity on the sensors?"

Flores was frantically flipping switches and pushing buttons. He said as he keyed the mic, "Blue Team, you getting this?"

Reynolds said back, "Yeah, sensors are going nuts but no visual activity I can see." Blue Team's drone signal vanished; in the Trench a violent explosion sent blinding light into the darkness, rocked the walls and sent a cascade of debris falling into the depths.

Then—all was still again.

Reynolds looked over to Sanderson. "Well hell, the surprise factor is gone. That's for sure. What do you want to do?"

Sanderson was still monitoring the sensors. "Standby here for a little while. Their drone made it through okay. Let's see what happens next before we make our move."

Reynolds nodded, keyed the mic and said, "Red Team, hold your position. Let's watch things for a while."

"Roger."

Chapter Eighty-Two

Flores sat monitoring his drone. He sat more upright and said, "I'm gonna try something." He flipped off several switches. "Damn... not a lot of maneuvering room down here. Let's try this..." he said and pulled back hard on the joystick that controlled the forward motion of the drone. "Come on baby... that's it baby... come on."

"What are you doing?" Kuriname asked.

"Barrel rolling the drone. I'm swinging back for another pass, but I'm shutting down the front and side sonar system. I'll leave the camera live and I'm slowing the speed." He started a slow side-to-side movement on the stick. "I'm using the thruster to 'swim' it, like a big fish." He looked over at Kuriname. "I'm playing a hunch... hold on."

On the view screen, the image was swinging side-to-side. Flores said, "Let me know when I'm getting close, check the GPS."

Kuriname tracked the drone; after a minute he said, "Getting close. Looks like 200 yards and closing."

"You got anything on the sensors?" Flores asked, slowing the drone even more.

"No, I'm not receiving any impulses from the Deep Star," Kuriname said. "Okay, fifty yards and closing. Forty yards and closing, thirty, twenty-five... fifteen... okay, we're even with the facility."

Flores was focused on the video screen and joystick. "Count off the distance as we pass it. Let me know if we get any response."

Kuriname watched the pip on the GPS. "Fifteen yards, twenty... thirty-five, forty, forty-five... fifty yards past the facility and still going."

Flores flipped the sonar back on and quit wiggling the joystick; the drone continued straight on its path. "Hmmm, still no response?"

Kuriname watched for several seconds before saying, "Nothing and we have rounded the cliff. The drone is safe."

"Roger," Flores said and keyed his mic. "Blue, did you just watch that?"

"Roger Red, I saw it. What are you thinking?" Reynolds asked.

Flores smiled into the mic. "I'm thinking the defenses did not recognize the drone as a threat this time. The speed and straight path of the drone on the first pass tripped the sensors and armed the system. My drone was out of range before it could launch, that's when yours came into view and got blasted. I turned off sonar, slowed mine way down this time, and wagged its tail from side-to-side," Flores said.

Reynolds said, "Like a fish? You swam past it?"

"Exactly."

"Interesting," Reynolds said.

"Very… patch in Comm for Sanderson and the Big Guy." He meant Michael Rourke.

Reynolds hit two switches and said, "Go ahead, Red."

"Okay, Gentlemen, I need some guidance here," Flores said. "We just made another pass at the target, this time slower, no sonar and I swam it like a fish... and nothing happened."

"What are you thinking?" Michael asked.

Flores took a deep breath. "I think I'm thinking the defense system was activated by the speed of the first pass and the sonar pings we were sending out. If I'm right, that means the system is on autopilot. That explains how our drone made it through the chute and yours didn't. It took a few seconds for the automatic system to energize, lock on target and destroy it."

Sanderson offered an idea. "What if it took a human monitor by surprise and that delayed him from responding in time to get both drones?"

Flores nodded and said, "That's a possibility. However, this time my drone swam slowly by. A human who launched on the first pass would already be on alert. Would have been watching, able to see the drone, identify it as a bogey and... he should have launched against it. I think the defenses are unmanned. Make sense to you?"

Sanderson said, "Give us a minute... Okay, let's say you're correct; what's the next step?"

Flores thought. "We have a GPS on the target. Let's approach from the top of the Trench and then slowly drift over the edge of the Trench and down. We turn off everything except propulsion, the video cameras and life support."

Michael said, "Give us a couple of minutes. I want to take a closer look at the video feedback."

"Roger that, Boss," Flores confirmed. "Red Team on standby."

Chapter Eighty-Three

Red and Blue teams moved to the top of the Trench above the target. The Comm link back to Captain Hasher was slow, slower than slow... finally he received the data he needed. "Red Team, listen closely," Hasher said. "During the battle at the underwater Russian city, we learned the location of their airlock hatches were protected, and away from their armaments and defenses. Since it and Deep Star were probably built at the same time or near to it, I don't think they would have changed something like this."

"Sir," Flores said. "I've talked to the people in Red One; we all have agreed to make the first try. After all, it's my idea so I don't want to put anyone else in the line of fire. My team is ready; let us see if I'm correct. If I can get down safely and find one of the airlocks, we can radio you and move everyone into position."

"And what if you're wrong?" Reynolds asked.

Flores said with a smile, "Then you don't get the hundred bucks you loaned me last month. What do you say, Sir?"

Michael took the mic from Reynolds. "Okay, Red One, make the first attempt, everyone else is on standby. Red One, if you don't make it, I'll give Blue One the hundred myself."

"Thanks Sir, but let's be a little more optimistic. What if I do make it?"

Michael smiled. "Then I'll promote you, Red One, and you can give the hundred back yourself."

"Roger that, Sir, I like your style. All units standby... Red One going down." He shut down the sonar system and slowly eased the throttle forward. Nearing the lip of the canyon, Flores angled the nose of the

MANTA down; drifting into the abyss. "Slowly... slowly..." he mumbled under his breath. Watching the dials and gauges, he said softly, "God, here we go. Watch over these men and our families. Let us do this right."

Then he was over the edge of the cliff and gone.

*****

As they slowly drifted downward, Kuriname asked Flores, "We're going to be facing Spetsnaz inside, right?"

Flores was monitoring all of the screens but he answered, "Yeah, but they're not indestructible. They're good, trained in everything from weapons and rappelling to diving and underwater combat."

Kuriname said, "I heard they had a midget sub called the 'Piranha'; carried six frogmen and their equipment and a two-man torpedo that was launched through an ordinary sub's torpedo tube, it had two warheads."

"Yeah," Flores said, still watching monitors, "and larger ones. The Triton-1 could carry two combat divers and Triton-2s carried six. Troopers used the APS Underwater Assault Rifle and the SPP-1 underwater pistol. The APS didn't use conventional bullets, too inaccurate and very short range underwater. It fired a steel bolt; the magazine held twenty-six rounds that were over four inches in length.

"The SPP-1 was better for close-up self-defense, not for attacking distant targets. Like the APS, it fired a sharpened steel bolt. At this depth, we won't see that kind of fight. If we run into them, it will be when we're in Deep Star. If the question is, what would Spetsnaz in this facility be using? The answer is... we don't know."

Kuriname nodded. "But we'll soon find out, right?"

Flores said nothing, he just watched the screens.

Chapter Eighty-Four

Michael Rourke hated sitting on the ledge waiting for Red One to report. *Hell,* he thought, *I might as well be in Honolulu.* But he saw the logic in what Flores was trying to do. *We just don't have enough Intel about this place. I know we can't and shouldn't rush headlong into a disaster but... I have to know if my father is here and still alive.*

*****

"You got anything on your monitors?" Flores asked as he manipulated the thrusting system on the MANTA and slowed to a hover.

Kuriname shook his head. "No, I'm getting low-level, electrical readings but nothing like a launch or weapons coming on line. How much further?"

"See that rock outcropping right there?"

Akiro looked up. "Yeah, I see it."

"Well, you better get ready, it's just below that." The tension inside the MANTA was electric; Flores heard the men behind him shifting positions to get ready... *Get ready for what?* he thought. Then they cleared the outcrop, there it was... massive! *Heavy steel, small view ports... four hundred meters long... at least,* Flores guessed. He saw torpedo tubes set to fire horizontally, missile silos set to fire vertically. "Research facility my ass," he said aloud. "It's a damn nuke base. Any readings? We are wide open if this thing wants to hit us."

Kuriname said, "No change... a trap?"

"Probably, let the rest of the force know what we have. I'm gonna hover here for a minute and see what happens. Look off to the right, look like a docking station to you?"

Kuriname was typing as fast as he could to send an ELF message to the rest of the team waiting above them. "Yeah, it does. Message sent."

"Good," Flores said. "Are we getting all of this recorded? If we get hit, I want the boys upstairs to know what they're walking into."

"Yeah, the recorders are in a constant ELF transmission mode."

"Okay, hang on guys," Flores said over his shoulder. "We're going in. Keep your fingers crossed."

Chapter Eighty-Five

The rocking chair beat a soft rhythmic tattoo on the floor as Sarah tried to lull Eddie to sleep. Emma, sitting on the overstuff couch said, "It is so quiet with the kids gone. So still."

Sarah smiled. "I know, I miss them already but I have to admit... I'm enjoying the quiet. No television, no music... It's exactly what I needed and exactly where I needed to be." She brushed a lock of hair back off her grandson's forehead. Frowning, she placed her hand on the baby's head and then his cheek. "Emma, come over here; is it me or does he have a temperature?"

Emma rose and put her hand on the baby. "No, it's not you. Let me get a thermometer." She returned, having fetched the thermometer from the medicine cabinet in the master bathroom and checked. "Yup, we have a temp... only a hundred right now. I thought he was acting a little cranky earlier. I'm going to give him some children's fever reducer," Emma said returning to the medicine cabinet.

After giving Eddie the proper dose, Emma said, "Probably nothing but we should watch it." Sarah hummed softly and began rocking the baby again.

Chapter Eighty-Six

Flores was taking his time, inching the MANTA toward the hatch. At any second he expected to be blown out of the water. Akiro Kuriname's uniform shirt was soaked with sweat; he continued to call out distances to Flores. "Twenty feet... fifteen... ten..."

Flores kicked the nose of the craft upright, and using belly cameras kept inching forward so the hatch on the bottom of the MANTA would align with Deep Star's hatch. *This is probably when we get destroyed.* He pushed the thought out of his head and focused on the alignment.

Kuriname said, "Five feet... contact in seven, six, five, four, three, two, one... contact." A clank reverberated through the MANTA. "Magnetic couplings... engaged, collar seal... confirmed. Initiating drain sequence... drain complete."

Flores wiped sweat from his face and sat back heavily in the pilot's chair. "Damn, we made it this far."

Kuriname's men had already activated their side of the airlock to stabilize pressure within the MANTA. "Alright, get ready... once we break this seal we have to open Deep Star's hatch. Be ready for anything. Switch to suit air, they could try to gas us when we open their hatch," Kuriname said, as he moved to the hatch and put on his face mask. He turned on his suit air before turning the wheel on the MANTA's hatch.

He grabbed the dog wheel, turned it and swung the hatch on its hinges. "Here we go, Gentlemen. Go hot." Selector switches were engaged, two of his troopers moved; one went low and the other high to cover the inside of Deep Star when Kuriname opened the hatch. The Deep Star's dog wheel didn't turn, he reset himself and tried again,

straining. Slowly, almost microscopically, it moved. "Damn they dog-
ged the hell out of this hatch," he said, more to himself than anybody
else. After the first few inches, the wheel spun freely, it was open.

Kuriname pushed against the hatch, to shove it inside the Deep Star;
it didn't budge. He put his shoulder to it and shoved, a creaking sound
came from the hinges as it swung open. One man mirrored the inside
of the airlock, collapsed the telescopic handle and stuck it into his belt.
The high man stepped inside the airlock, rifle at the ready. "Clear."

Kuriname stepped into the airlock, looked out the small portal in the
door, nothing... no one to be seen. Walking to the control panel, all
indicators showed green. At the last gauge, he nodded. "Air pressure
normal on the other side of the door. I'm cracking it... now." The hatch
opened... no one was there.

"Caution men, let's find the bastards," Kuriname said. The Dog
Soldiers formed up on the other side of that hatch. Slowly, carefully,
they moved down the passageway to an intersection twenty feet away.
Again using the mirror they checked the new passageway in both directions. Kuriname and four men went left; the last four set up as rear
security walking backwards down the passageway, rifles at the ready
for any threat from that direction.

Kuriname noticed he could see his men's foot prints in a fine layer
of dust on the deck. He frowned. The only sound was the quiet hum of
machinery. He turned off his suit air and spat out his mouth piece, keying his throat mic. "Red One to Blue One, over."

"Go ahead, Red One."

"Zero contact so far. Bring down the cover ships and move your
MANTA left of ours; there's another airlock about fifty feet from the
one we used. See if you can gain entrance there and work your way
toward us, over."

"Roger, Blue One out."

Kuriname turned to his team. "Let's go off of suit air, conserve it. Hold here; let Blue Team dock before we go any further. This is..." He thought for a moment. "This is damn weird... damn weird and I don't like it. Eyes and ears open!"

Chapter Eighty-Seven

Sarah had checked Eddie's temperature three more times; each time it kept climbing, 102 now. "Emma," she called. "Have you made contact with the doctor yet?"

"Yes," Emma said as she walked back to Sarah. "He said it is not normal for a temperature to be climbing that quickly. Give him to me and grab your purse, we're going to meet him at the ER." Emma had called her father, and told him what was going on. Tim contacted the Secret Service agents parked outside; they moved down to the Rourke home to provide an escort to the hospital.

*****

Fifteen minutes later, Blue Team's MANTA had docked at the other airlock. Five minutes later, Michael Rourke keyed his throat mic. "Red One, this is Blue One, over."

"Go ahead Blue, over."

"We are inside Deep Star, so far... not seeing anything. Moving toward you, over."

Kuriname checked the panel on his left wrist, a display with two red dots showing. The stationary dot marked his location, the other was moving. "Roger, Blue One, out." Five minutes went by, Kuriname and his men had not encountered anyone or anything. They had heard no shots or sounds of attack on the other team. "Blue One, this is Red One, over."

"Go ahead, Red One, over."

"Looks like we are right in front of you, around the next corner, over."

"Roger, we're watching for you, out." A mirror flashed around the corner and the two teams linked up in the deserted passageway.

"Did you see anything, Michael?" Kuriname asked.

"Nothing." Michael shook his head. "Did your people?"

Kuriname shook his head. "Nothing."

"Is it possible this place is deserted?" Sanderson asked.

"Could be, or they are still hiding," Kuriname said.

Sanderson keyed his throat mic. "Chief Reynolds, what do you think about turning on more systems and see if you can get us a location on any personnel locations? Over."

Reynolds said, "It's alright with me, what do you think Flores? Over."

"Might as well, I'm not getting anything; let's switch on and see if we can find them. Over."

"Roger that, activating sensors, now." Quickly scanning his monitors, Reynolds added, "Nothing... I've got nothing here. Flores, you see anything? Over."

Flores fiddled with a couple of dials. "I'm not sure, give me a minute... I've got something but I can't tell for sure what it is. Blue One, there is something on the opposite side of the bulkhead in front and down to the right of you; can you see anything? Over."

Sanderson gave the signal for his men to shift positions; he pulled his mirror and checked in both directions. Nothing, he readied his rifle and stepped around into the next passageway. Thirty feet down the passageway was another airlock hatch.

Peering through the small portal, Michael said, "Holy crap!"

Chapter Eighty-Eight

The lead Secret Service car cleared a path through traffic with it lights and siren. Sarah followed closely, driving Emma's car while Emma rocked Eddie, wiping his face with a wet rag. Emma looked at Sarah. "Hurry please, he's burning up." Sarah kept her eyes on the road ahead but nodded... and said a silent prayer. *Please God, not the baby... not the baby, too.*

At the emergency room door, Sarah slid to a screeching stop behind the lead car; doctors and nurses with a gurney rushed the car. A nurse took Eddie from Emma, saying, "Please, let me have him, we have to hurry." Emma ran to follow her.

Sarah, flanked by the two Secret Service agents, hurried after them as she dialed Paul's number. "Paul, this is Sarah. We're at the hospital, it's Eddie. You better get everyone here." She heard another screech of tires and turning saw Tim Shaw running for the entrance, his car rolling slowly forward into a large concrete planter. He had forgotten to put it in park.

Chapter Eighty-Nine

Michael tried the hatch but it seemed locked from the inside. He motioned to one of the Dog Soldiers. "Can you just get the hinges off?"

The man named Allensby, looked at the hatch and said, "Sir, it won't do any good; even with the hinges gone, the bars dogging the hatch will still hold it in place. But..." he said, tapping the bulkhead, "I can cut a hole in this."

"Do it," Sanderson said. "Everybody on suit air, we can't be sure what the atmosphere is on the other side." Allensby pulled packets from two pockets on his assault vest, unrolled and connected two coils of something that looked like silver play dough, stretching and sticking them in a large rectangular pattern on the bulkhead. From another pocket he pulled out a switch with a wire hanging from it. He stuck the wire into the play dough. "Turn you heads and close your eyes, this is going to get hot and bright."

With a click and hiss, the silver play dough ignited, burning with incredible light, melting the steel of the bulkhead. When the cut was made, Allensby stepped back; a front kick sent the section of the wall across the inside of the room. Then he inserted a gauge, pushed a button and told Sanderson, "Air's good Sir."

Michael nodded, they switched off suit air and he stepped through the gaping hole, into a nightmare.

*****

Paul and Annie arrived first, they were sitting with Sarah when Natalia came running in. Sarah stood and held out her arms, Natalia took her in hers. "What... what happened, Sarah?"

"Eddie," Sarah said. "We noticed a fever, we kept checking it, but it started climbing. Very quickly. Emma called the doctor and we came right over. Tim is with Emma, they have Eddie in the pediatric ICU. Natalia, I'm scared; I'm scared it might be that plague. That God-awful, damn plague."

Chapter Ninety

"How is this possible?" Michael asked. "I saw bodies through the portal, complete bodies. Not this."

Kuriname said, "I suspect that they died long ago, a very long time ago. Nothing disturbed them until we gained entrance. It may have been a slight change in air pressure, the cutting flame or even the panel when it crashed in. When the vibrations reached the bodies, they disintegrated."

"How long do you think they've been dead?" someone in back asked.

Kuriname shook his head. "Maybe as far back as the Night of the War."

Michael examined the remains, now nothing more than dust and disarticulated bones. With a gloved hand, he swept an area near one of the bodies and picked up something; a metal identification tag, Russian. Natalia had taught him to read a little Russian. "Gentlemen, meet Colonel Lennart Schuback, commander of this facility." Moving from one pile of dust to another then another, he gathered other tags, "And meet Commander Bengt Rudberg, Senior Arms Specialist; Commander Emil Avsukjevitj, Section 1 Marine Spetsnaz; Colonel Anatoilij Michajlovitj, Communist Party Political Officer; and lastly, Subaltern Officers Pavel Besedin and Vasilij Savtjenko, junior officers. These identification tags were issued upon their posting to Deep Star, in 1979 for a tour of two years. The Night of the War beat them out of going home."

Michael turned to Akiro Kuriname. "I think we will find more of these people but few answers. We won't find what we came here for. He was never here. Where the hell is my father?"

Epilogue

"We'll find him Michael. We will find John Rourke, if we have to scour the entire planet. And we'll bring him home."

Michael looked at his friend, his very new friend who had once tried to kill or capture him. He thought of the original Akiro Kuriname, an old friend who he had fought alongside so long ago. The man this one had been cloned from.

Michael smiled and nodded but said, "What if we can't? What if we can't find him, everyone thought he'd be here. No one had another plan or possibility. Now we're back to zero; zero clues, zero options. What if we do find him and he's dead?"

Akiro recognized the strain in Michael's voice, now tinged from fear and anguish. "Then we will fight on, Michael. We'll fight for several things: to live, to be free, to make our own decisions and to pass on a better world than we found to our children. I asked your father once, what was the last line of freedom's defense? He smiled and said, 'Why, it is all of us.'"

*****

Tim Shaw walked slowly out into the waiting room; Paul saw him first and stood. Tim moved slowly almost like he was in a trance and he looked so incredibly... old. Halfway down the hallway, he looked up at Paul; at first he didn't see him and when he did... he didn't recognize him.

Recognition came to Shaw's face and he looked into Paul's eyes, slowly shook his head, turned around and went back to be with a grieving daughter. He mumbled to himself, "Never had a chance. Never had a chance, poor little angel. Never had a damned chance; damn plague."

Paul turned to Annie; tears ran down both cheeks as she held Sarah who simply, delicately sobbed. Paul looked at Natalia; she couldn't hold his gaze and turned away. For the first time in a long time, Paul felt alone... alone and as afraid as he had been that day so long ago when he first met John Rourke.

He thought, *John... John where are you? Where the hell are you?* Rourke's words came to him: "Sometimes, Paul, you have to do something, even if it might be wrong." Paul dialed his cell phone. "Otto, please come to the hospital. We need you... I need you to come."

Fifteen minutes later, Croenberg walked into the waiting room; he stopped, "Gott im Hemmel; what has happened?" Then he walked slowly to Rubenstein, nodded then knelt in front of Sarah. She looked up and smiled, one brief, painful smile, before the sobbing started again.